Dear Romance Reader,

Welcome to a world of breathtaking passion and never-ending romance.
Welcome to *Precious Gem Romances*.

It is our pleasure to present *Precious Gem Romances*, a wonderful new line of romance books by some of America's best-loved authors. Let these thrilling historical and contemporary romances sweep you away to far-off times and places in stories that will dazzle your senses and melt your heart.

Sparkling with joy, laughter, and love, each *Precious Gem Romance* glows with all the passion and excitement you expect from the very best in romance. Offered at a great affordable price, these books are an irresistible value—and an essential addition to your romance collection. Tender love stories you will want to read again and again, *Precious Gem Romances* are books you will treasure forever.

Look for fabulous new *Precious Gem Romances* each month—available only at Wal★Mart.

Kate Duffy
Editorial Director

THE COWBOY AND THE CRADLE

Becky Barker

Zebra Books
Kensington Publishing Corp.

http://www.zebrabooks.com

ZEBRA BOOKS are published by

Kensington Publishing Corp.
850 Third Avenue
New York, NY 10022

First Printing: April, 2000
10 9 8 7 6 5 4 3 2 1

Printed in the United States of America

This one's for our firstborn, Rachel, and her husband, Jerramy McCabe, with lots of love and best wishes for a long, happy marriage.

One

"Don't look now, but The King has arrived. And he's alone."

Katlyn Sanders faced Ryan Havens as he looked toward the entrance of the shelter house. Her back was to the door, so she couldn't see the latest arrival at the Labor Day festivities.

She felt his presence, though; instantly and painfully. Just knowing he was close made the blood rush through her veins and kicked her pulse into overdrive.

She'd known Jared King would be here today, known she'd have to face him for the first time since walking out on him. She'd thought herself prepared, but her stomach muscles clenched in sudden panic.

"Twelve seconds. That's how long it took his eyes to find you," her companion drawled.

Katlyn acknowledged Ryan's comment with a weak smile. She could have argued that she'd felt Jared's eyes on her in ten seconds flat, but why quibble?

"What's he got that I haven't got?" asked her lifelong pal. "What causes the stir of excitement when he enters a crowd? What is it about him that draws every woman's attention and rouses the envy of every other male in the place?"

Katlyn managed a more natural smile. Ryan had the same effect on people hereabouts, but was oblivious of the fact.

"Are you asking or are you about to tell me?" she teased, forcing a lightness to her tone that she didn't begin to feel.

He ignored the interruption. "King and I are both responsible, respected members of the community. Both intelligent, successful and wealthy. He may be a couple inches taller, but I'm twice as good-looking, aren't I?"

Ryan was a blond, blue-eyed Adonis. Jared King's roughly hewn features were more rugged than handsome. There was no real contest in the looks department.

"You are definitely one gorgeous guy," she insisted, eyes dancing.

Ryan gave her a slow smile, then his tone dropped to an intimate grumble. "So why does his proximity make that little pulse flutter in your throat, bring a blush to your cheeks and make your eyes sparkle like emeralds?"

Katlyn's hand involuntarily slipped to her throat. Her gaze locked with Ryan's. His flippant questions could not conceal the underlying seriousness in his tone.

She desperately wished she could return his unfaltering love. He was such a good man, and the platonic devotion she felt for him was not what he wanted or needed.

"If I could control it, I'd change it in a heartbeat," she swore softly.

Ryan gazed into her eyes a moment longer, nodded his acceptance of her edict, then shifted his attention to the collection of townspeople in the building. Most had already eaten from the food-laden tables, and several conversations were in full swing.

Jared King exchanged greetings with friends and neighbors as he slowly but steadily made his way towards them.

"He doesn't look too cheerful. Do you think he'll cause a scene?"

Katlyn tucked a lock of her shoulder-length hair behind her ear. She didn't know what to expect, and the suspense was making her nerves tap dance to a riotous tune.

Jared wasn't a predictable man. He might demand an explanation. He might rant and rave. Or he might just act as though her leaving didn't faze him in the least.

Whatever his plan of action, it would wound her. There was no way to avoid the pain at this stage.

"Want me to defend your honor?"

"No," she admonished softly. The last sip of her cola partially eased the sudden dryness of her throat. "If you're itching for a fight, forget it." She didn't want the two men she loved most in the world fighting over her.

Ryan grimaced. "What if he gets mean?"

A flood of intimate, unwelcome memories washed over Katlyn, making the blood sing through her veins. Jared was a big and powerful man, but with the power came the awesome strength to control it.

He was a man of intense passions, yet he'd always been incredibly gentle and protective of her. He might have an inherent mistrust of women, but his deeply felt sense of honor ensured that he'd never use his physical strength to hurt someone smaller or more vulnerable.

"He won't hurt me. He's probably going to thank me for leaving him before he had to throw me out."

"Yeah, right." Her companion's clipped tone and tight expression mocked her words. "He's making his way straight to you, darlin'. Want me to stay close or get lost?"

Katlyn was torn. She dreaded the thought of being alone with Jared, even amidst a crowd of their friends and neighbors. But she had no right to ask Ryan to run interference for her.

"I'll have to face him sooner or later."

When all the fine hairs on her neck were prickling with sensation, she knew Jared was getting close. At Ryan's nod, she turned and faced her former lover as the two men exchanged greetings.

"King."

"Havens."

They were civil, but not much more.

Jared's undivided, unnerving attention riveted on Katlyn. He was a head taller than her five-foot-five, so she lifted her eyes to his. The wide breadth of his shoulders blocked everyone else from view.

His greeting for her was similar to the one for Ryan, but his tone lost the hostility and became neutral.

"Katlyn."

The deep baritone touched her in ways no other could manage. She searched his features for some clue to his mood, but the hard angles and planes were devoid of emotion. Her pulse thudded heavily in her ears, and her emotions were in such turmoil that she barely trusted her voice.

"Hello, Jared."

Eyes nearly as dark as his ebony hair made a brief but probing study of her face. Her heart raced. She wasn't sure what he was searching for, but hoped her expression was as unrevealing as his.

She knew his eyes could go as cold and hard as granite, or as hot as liquid fire. They could also guard his thoughts as coolly as they were doing now.

"We need to talk."

Panic flared briefly, and Katlyn looked to Ryan. She was tempted to use him as an emotional shield, but sanity reigned. Instead, she offered him a tight smile of reassurance and reluctant dismissal.

As Ryan walked away, the tension grew thick and suffocating, making Katlyn's nerves raw. She tried to tell herself it would ease in time.

"Let's go somewhere more private."

They were standing in a quiet corner of the huge old shelter. People were slowly making their way outside to participate in horseshoe tournaments and baseball and volleyball games organized for the energetic.

Bingo and progressive euchre were being played by those who preferred more sedate games. In another hour or so, at dusk, music and dancing would be an added attraction.

"You haven't eaten yet," she hedged.

"I'm not hungry," he insisted, but the look that fleetingly entered his eyes was ravenous. It suggested a totally different kind of hunger.

Katlyn felt fire licking along her veins. Until she'd

walked out on him two weeks ago, they'd been passionate, insatiable lovers.

After twenty-two years of nearly virtuous existence, she'd shocked herself and the entire community of Kingston by moving in with Jared. He'd asked her to, and she'd agreed. The decision had been momentous for someone who'd never challenged the rules of small town conservatism.

As a child, she'd been taught to color inside the lines. She'd even gone so far as to trace the lines so that she didn't venture beyond propriety. All that had changed when she met Jared.

For her, it had been love at first sight. She'd never met anyone who made her feel the way he did; so alive, so special, so complete. Fairy tales of happily-ever-after had seemed within her reach. She'd fallen hard and fast.

Katlyn had assumed the feeling was mutual, but she'd been wrong. Although Jared had been totally unselfish in every other aspect of their relationship, he'd never shared his real self with her. Never shared his private thoughts, feelings and dreams.

She shifted her gaze to the soda can she was holding, needing to concentrate on something mundane, and hoping he didn't notice how her hand trembled as she tossed the can in a recycling bin.

"We can go out to the ranch."

"No!" She heard the alarm in her tone, and forced herself to stay calm. "There's no reason we can't talk right here."

Jared glanced around them. Too many people were too interested in their exchange. "Let's walk down to the stream," he suggested.

The narrow stream behind the community park

was off limits for games and all the younger citizens. The overhanging willows along its bank would provide some privacy from curious eyes.

Katlyn nodded and turned toward the back entrance of the shelter house. Jared stepped closer and touched a guiding hand to the back of her waist. His fingers seared her flesh through the cotton blouse, sending little sparks of fire throughout her body.

She grew more apprehensive as they headed away from the noisy crowd and closer to the secluded, tree-lined stream. She had no fear of Jared, only a fear of her own weakness where he was concerned.

She knew this confrontation was necessary and wanted it behind her. She dreaded the inevitable arguments, but mostly she prayed for the strength to convince him they were finished even though she loved him more than life itself.

When they came to a stop on the grassy bank of the stream, Katlyn shifted from his touch and turned to face him. Jeans and cotton shirts were the standard attire in this area, and they were similarly dressed. But she couldn't help notice how dangerously sexy Jared looked in close-fitting jeans that hugged his strong thighs and . . . the wayward direction of her thoughts scattered with his next words.

"Gossip has it that I threw you out of my house," he began in a voice rough with accusation.

Heat suffused Katlyn's cheeks. She leaned down and picked up a small twig to momentarily conceal her discomfort. Then she toyed with it restlessly while settling her back against a broad tree trunk. Finally, she found the courage to face him squarely.

"Everyone figured you'd throw me out sooner or later. I didn't offer any explanations. They'll all believe what they want anyway."

Jared uttered a harsh oath. "Our relationship is nobody's business!"

Katlyn agreed. "I know that, but we both grew up in Kingston. People here think of themselves as extended family with the right to pass judgment on everything and anything they choose."

"You can't let the whole world control your personal life," he insisted, not for the first time. "Did someone say something to you? If you were harassed or insulted, just tell me who's responsible, and I'll make sure it never happens again."

She shook her head sadly. He just didn't get it. "There's nothing you can do. You might be a pillar of the community, but you can't stop the gossip and you can't change generations of moral standards."

"Tell me what happened," Jared demanded in frustration. "Why the hell did you leave?"

"I explained my feelings a dozen times. You just refused to accept the fact that I was serious." She'd gone while he was working, too distraught to fight him if he tried to coax her to stay. She'd wanted a clean break and time to rebuild her defenses.

"Just 'bye, it's been nice, but I'm leaving,' " he grumbled.

"What more was there to say, Jared?" she beseeched him with wounded eyes. "We both knew it was a temporary arrangement. I'm hopelessly old-fashioned. I had a strict upbringing, and I was never comfortable being a live-in lover, significant other, or whatever the currently popular term is."

"We're lovers whether we live together or not,"

he countered, tension evident in every line of his big body. "Living with me is just more open and honest than most people can stand."

"Aunt Trudy is one of those people," she reminded him about the woman who'd been both mother and father to her since her parents' untimely deaths. As much as she loved Jared, she hated hurting and disappointing her aunt.

Living in sin, as Trudy Sanders called it, was like a slap in the face to the woman who'd done everything humanly possible to raise her properly.

"Is she the reason you left? Is she happier now that you're back at her place?" he asked.

"Things are still a little tense between us, but we're both trying."

"Did you let her believe I'd thrown you out?" Jared's tone and expression grew more fierce. "That should really convince her I'm a worthless bastard, shouldn't it?"

Katlyn blushed guiltily. Jared didn't spend a lot of time worrying about what other people thought of him, but he had made an effort with her aunt Trudy.

"I'm sorry about that. I told her the truth, but I don't know if she really believed me."

"Maybe she'll believe it and accept it when you move back home where you belong."

"Trudy's house in town is my home. I'm not moving back to your ranch."

Jared's jaws clenched, and his fists were clenched at his sides. The telltale signs made Katlyn wonder if he was just angry that she dared refuse him or if he was feeling the same chaotic mix of emotions she was suffering.

She knew he cared. He'd shown her in a hundred different ways. For a while, she'd convinced herself that the caring and passion could evolve into the kind of wholehearted love she felt for him. Now she wondered if he was capable of that kind of giving.

When Jared spoke again, his tone was grim. "So, did you decide that living at the infamous King Ranch wasn't quite the life of luxury you expected?"

Katlyn knew the question was hard for him to ask. He thought his money and social status were what women found most attractive about him. In part, he was asking if that's all that had attracted her, too.

"I never expected luxury, Jared, but I didn't expect to be alone twelve to fourteen hours a day, either."

"I have a ranch to run. I'm not one of the idle rich, regardless of what people think. The ranch is prosperous enough, but the lawsuits have drained my cash reserves. I thought I made that clear."

His ongoing legal battles were a major part of their problem. Jared's dad had been married several times. One of the cast-off spouses had thought herself entitled to a bigger chunk of King property and money.

So far, Jared had managed to win the suits, but the cost of the legal battles, both financially and emotionally, had been devastating.

Money wasn't an issue between them. Katlyn wasn't interested in his wealth. But Jared's contempt for marriage *was* a major issue. He'd made it clear that he'd never marry, and she'd tried to make it clear that she couldn't accept anything less.

"It's the same old impasse, Jared," she whispered

softly. "I accept your feelings on the subject, but you refuse to accept mine. I can't handle being a 'kept woman.' "

"Maybe you just didn't like the style you were being kept in," he suggested smoothly, his eyes full of dark cynicism. "Well, I can't afford a full-time cook and housekeeper right now, and I can't afford expensive entertaining. Money's tight, but it won't always be that way."

Katlyn shook her head again, causing heavy waves of satiny dark hair to rock around her face. Jared clung to the notion that wealth and its trimmings were important to all women. Even her.

"I don't have expensive tastes, and I'm not much of a party animal," she reminded him gently.

"Then what's wrong with my place? You said you loved the house, the entertainment system, the pool and all the fancy kitchen gadgets."

She had loved his home, but not rattling around in it by herself. He worked long hours and refused to let her help with ranch chores. She was a trained chef and loved cooking for him, but too many meals had been ruined while she waited, waited, waited.

"I can't stand being idle, Jared. I'm used to being busy and productive." And communicating. She'd never thought of herself as an extrovert, but she hadn't much cared for seemingly endless hours and days of her own company.

She'd have loved the ranch life if he'd spent more time just talking with her, sharing his thoughts and concerns, or if he'd tried to make her feel a part of his ranch family.

Instead, their time together had been spent making love and little else. The memories brought a resurgence of warmth to her body, but she swiftly quelled her wayward thoughts.

"You'd rather be slaving over a stove at the restaurant?" he snapped, tone and stance aggressive.

Katlyn bristled. "I've always enjoyed my work, so don't make it sound like it's the lowest job on earth."

"I didn't mean to do that," he argued. "I thought you'd be happy to get a break from it. You've worked for your aunt most of your life."

"Well, you've worked on the ranch most of your life," she countered defensively. "Just because the situations are different, doesn't mean that my work is less important to me. I should never have let you talk me into giving it up in the first place."

Jared grimaced and raked his hand through his hair in frustration. "So move back home and keep your job if it's that important to you."

"I can't live with you and face my aunt's hurt and disapproval every day."

He cursed under his breath, turned and paced the short distance to the water. Katlyn watched warily, wondering what his next move would be. She had to remain firm, but she knew that the least little sign that anything besides his pride was hurting could destroy all her defenses.

When he finally turned back to her, his eyes were narrowed and calculating. She knew he'd reinforced his defenses rather than given in to emotions he would consider a weakness. His attitude helped stiffen her resolve.

"So what do you want? Is this some kind of game I'm supposed to understand?" he demanded, moving closer again. "If you're holding out for a wedding band, then you'd better tell it to me straight. Did you leave just to see if you could make me change my mind?"

Katlyn's eyes were big and sad as she studied his lean features. "I'm not playing games, Jared. We tried and failed. It's over."

Anger flared again in his eyes. Then they were shuttered with dark lashes. Tension pulsed like a wild thing between them. He didn't argue, just slowly stepped closer. Katlyn's back was pressed against the tree trunk, and his big body shifted within inches of hers.

He didn't immediately touch her, but the familiar scent of him enveloped her. It set her blood aflame and evoked erotic memories of tightly entwined bodies and incredibly sensual delights.

Her gaze never wavered from his as he plucked the mangled twig from her nervous fingers and tossed it aside. She lowered her lashes to conceal her reaction when he laced his long, work-roughened fingers with her smaller, softer ones. Then he lifted both her hands to his mouth. When he placed a warm, gentle kiss on each, the breath hissed from her lungs in a rush.

Their gazes met; his taunting, hers wary. She'd imagined all sorts of reactions from him, but she hadn't anticipated a soft, tender assault on her senses.

"How can you even pretend it's over between us?" he wanted to know, his voice a deep, sexy tone of wounded arrogance. "Just being this close sets both of us on fire. The passion isn't going to die a natural death. It's alive and burning as hot as ever."

Katlyn tried to concentrate on drawing air into

her lungs She wished his words were less true. She truly believed their relationship was destined for failure. Their wants and needs were too diverse. Prolonging it was a terrible mistake, yet her body refused to listen to logic.

It had been like this since the first time he'd taken her in his arms. Her brain screamed warnings and lectures of propriety that her heart and body unfailingly chose to ignore.

"Tell me you don't want me," Jared insisted in a gruff whisper.

His lips brushed hers with a butterfly kiss guaranteed to tantalize. He inched close enough to trap their hands between their bodies, then he continued to nibble on her mouth and murmur seductively.

"Tell me you never want to kiss me again, never want my hands on you, never want to make love with me again."

A familiar, melting warmth flowed through Katlyn's veins, made her knees grow weak and her body begin to ache. Jared was the first and only lover she'd ever known. He'd been an uninhibited, insatiable tutor. Her body remembered every single, thrilling lesson.

TWO

"Convince me, Katie," Jared demanded as his mouth roved from her lips to the erratically throbbing pulse at her throat.

He nibbled, and she shivered.

"Tell me you can't stand my touch and that your body doesn't ache for mine. Convince me, and I'll know it's really over."

Katlyn tried. She really tried to say the words that would make her feelings clear, but her throat was constricted, and she couldn't find her voice. Her blood was roaring in her ears, her body trembling. When he took a step closer and pressed his lower body against hers, it was all she could do to remain upright.

There was no denying his arousal. Despite the heavy denim of their jeans, his desire was blatantly obvious; a virile and insistent measure of his masculinity.

The strength of his need had always amazed her. She couldn't understand why he found her exciting. She'd never considered herself sexy or beautiful or desirable, yet there was no doubting that he did. His hunger was a heady aphrodisiac.

"Jared, we need to talk."

Her half-hearted attempt to distract him was

wasted. He ignored her, putting his mouth to work in a more effective manner. He caressed her neck with hot kisses and then a slow, sucking action that made her toes curl and heat spiral to the pit of her stomach.

All the while, he was slowly rubbing the evidence of his arousal against the softness of her stomach and heightening her arousal, too. A needy sob escaped.

It seemed like years instead of weeks since she'd felt so alive, so hungry. She'd missed him more than she'd ever imagined possible. She knew it was wrong to succumb to his deliberate seduction, but it felt so good, so right to have him close again.

Jared used their joined hands to gently stroke her breasts until the nipples were rigid and tingling with wanton sensation. His lips slid back to hers and took them with tightly leashed hunger. His tongue thrust inside her mouth with the same slow, gyrating rhythm that his thighs made against the softness of hers.

Katlyn ached with need. She felt totally at Jared's mercy; a toy he was playing with; a game he was determined to win. She was in way over her head.

Then the unexpected happened. His considerable control snapped, stunning her. In all their hours, and days, and weeks of lovemaking, he'd never lost control. That's what had finally convinced her she was nothing more than a passing fancy in his life. But now she felt convulsive shudders racking his body and she began to tremble herself.

He shifted still closer so that his strong thighs were pressing her tightly against the tree. His arms felt like bands of steel as he clutched her against his chest while deepening the kiss until neither of them could breathe.

His mouth was hot, wet and ravenous. He kissed her relentlessly, sweeping his tongue into her mouth and filling it with the taste of him. The world stood still as he kissed her again and again until they were both weak and shaky.

Katlyn returned his kisses as best she could, trying to satisfy some of his primitive hunger. She knew he was hurting as badly as she was. After a month of living together and sating themselves with each other, they were both suffering from withdrawal. She understood and wished there was a better way to handle the situation, but they seemed incapable of compromise.

He wanted her to live with him indefinitely, but he had no desire for a wife and family. The weeks she'd lived with him had taught her a lot about herself. She was a woman of deep passion and a deep capacity to love. Her feelings for him could easily become obsessive. She wanted it all; a husband, lover and father for her children.

They would never agree, and continuing the relationship was just wrong. She knew it—she just had to convince him. But she couldn't say the words that he promised would bring it to an end. Nor, apparently, could she resist him.

When one of Jared's muscled thighs eased between hers, Katlyn's legs involuntary clenched around it. A fiery liquid heat accompanied by an insistent throbbing heightened her arousal to a fever pitch.

Her low, keening moan brought a deep groan from Jared and a powerful flexing of his thigh muscle. He dragged his mouth from hers, but continued the sensual onslaught. His lips seared her ultra-sensitive skin as they left her lips to burn a path down her cheek and neck until settling with unerring accuracy on a taut nipple.

He teased the peak to painful rigidity through layers of clothing. When he grew impatient with the fabric barrier, his mouth nuzzled inside her blouse. He eased his grip on her long enough to flip the hook of her bra, then dropped his hands to her hips to pull her closer. As he lifted her higher, his mouth fastened on tender, bare flesh.

He sucked at Katlyn's breast, drawing the nipple deeply into his mouth while she clutched his head and fought for breath.

"Jared!" she gasped, her voice a ragged whisper.

In response, he shifted his attention to the other breast, his mouth latching onto the pebbled tip. Katlyn moaned and pressed her head back against the tree while her fingers and toes curled in reaction.

Jared's breathing was as erratic as hers. The evidence of his desire pulsed at the cradle of her thighs, demanding attention. Katlyn knew he was rapidly reaching the point of no return. She wished she could give him the physical release he needed without the emotional tangles, but it was no use.

His frustration was blatant and physical. Hers was far more complex and all tangled up with propriety, loyalties and years of social conditioning. She didn't seem to be capable of saying no to him; didn't want to say no, yet it hurt too much to say yes. It hurt more than she'd ever imagined possible.

She wasn't aware of the tears streaming down her

cheeks until Jared abruptly ended their kiss. His head jerked backwards as if she'd slapped him. The harshness of his breathing echoed in her ears.

The hot passion in his eyes dimmed a little as he eased his grip on her and stared, stunned by the evidence of her pain.

"I hurt you." His tone was heavy with self-disgust. "I didn't mean to be so rough."

"No," she contended, swiping the embarrassing wetness from her cheeks with trembling fingers. She had very little pride left where he was concerned, but she wasn't the type to use tears to get her way. "You've never physically hurt me."

Jared turned his back on her. He raked a hand through his hair and paced in frustration. Katlyn let out a ragged sigh. She watched him, knowing he needed a few minutes to regain control. She tried to do the same, but tensed when he finally turned and speared her with his dark, angry eyes.

"What's this all about, Katlyn? If it's a ploy for a wedding ring, then it's a waste of time. You aren't the first woman who's ever tried to coerce me into marriage, and it won't work for you any more than it did for them. I thought you understood that."

"I do," she assured him, eyes beseeching. "I understand how you feel and why you feel that way. I even thought for a while that I could ignore my own wants and needs in order to satisfy yours, but I found out I'm more selfish than that. I don't want to settle for being any man's mistress. If you can't trust me enough to make me your wife, then we have no future."

"So you decided to torture me and then issue an ultimatum?" he suggested savagely.

"No." Anger swiftly dried her tears and stiffened her spine. She didn't care for the picture he was painting or his impression of her standards.

She stood tall and returned his angry glare. "I don't want anything from you. Period. No ultimatums, no guilt trips, no games. We tried and it didn't work. It's over. Nothing is going to change that now."

"Why? Because Ryan Havens is willing to give you what I won't? Because his financial status is a little more secure than mine right now? Does a future with him suddenly look more appealing?"

Katlyn stiffened. "That's a mean thing to suggest!" she countered. "For your information, I could have married Ryan years ago if I wanted to. I wish I loved him enough to even consider a future as his wife."

"Love?" Jared snarled the word. "You swore you loved me enough to share my life. What happened to all your whispered promises of forever love? What's your declaration of love really worth? Nothing."

"I never said I stopped loving you!" Katlyn argued, her tone furious and resentful.

"Well you have a hell of a way of showing it," he snapped.

"How would you know?" she challenged hotly. "You've never loved anything in your life except that ranch. You're too hardhearted and proud to allow yourself any finer feelings. You don't have the emotional capacity for a long-term commitment."

Once started, she couldn't seem to control the hot flow of words. "You made your feelings on the subject very clear while I was with you, and I decided what you had to offer wasn't enough. It has nothing to do with my love for you.

"In fact," she continued, "loving you just made me all that more determined to have a real, meaningful relationship with someone else. If I can't have what I want with you, then I'll keep looking until I find a man who can offer it all to me."

"And you'll conveniently learn to love him, too?"

His contempt pierced her heart like a knife; wounding deeply and deflating her anger. Katlyn conceded defeat. Trying to make him understand her decision was useless. She already knew that, so why was she beating her head against a brick wall?

He came from a hopelessly dysfunctional family that had jaded his view of everything. He didn't trust many women and trusted the institution of marriage even less. He had good reason to be wary. She understood that. Her mistake was in believing, like a naïve twit, that her love could change his attitude.

Jared didn't love her. Maybe he wasn't capable of the depth of feeling she wanted and needed from him. Maybe he wouldn't recognize the finer feelings even if they hit him square in the heart.

"So far, I haven't been too thrilled with the throes of true love, either," she said derisively. Her fingers trembled as she straightened her clothing, but her voice was firm again. "I'm not so anxious to experiment with it anymore just now."

Jared speared her with narrowed eyes. "So what's Havens to you?"

"My best friend," she replied. "He's been my best friend since grade school. I don't expect that to change anytime soon."

"He wants to be a whole lot more than a friend."

Katlyn didn't deny it. "My relationship with Ryan really isn't any of your business."

It was obvious that Jared didn't care for her words or her tone, yet there wasn't a thing he could do about it. He had no legal or moral hold over her, and she was doing her best to break the emotional hold.

Twilight was falling, and it was obviously time to bring their discussion to an end and get back to the celebration. She tucked her blouse more neatly into her jeans and tried to smooth her hair, hoping she didn't look as disheveled as she felt.

"What now?" Jared demanded. "Are we just supposed to pretend there's nothing between us?"

"I figure we can ignore that physical attraction if we just don't get too close to each other."

His bark of laughter mocked her words. "You think the hunger will ease? This is the first time we've seen each other in two weeks, but the desire wasn't any less urgent, was it?"

Katlyn turned her back on his deliberate taunting and started up the path toward the shelter house. She knew it wasn't going to be easy for them to ignore each other, but it could be done.

"Our paths rarely cross on a regular basis," she reminded him. "We both work long hours and have little time for socializing. We won't have to see each other that often."

"And what if I have no intention of accepting your decision?" drawled Jared, moving close to her and putting a guiding hand at her waist again.

His words were as unsettling as his touch. Katlyn was perversely pleased and alarmed by his attitude.

She didn't know how she could resist him on a regular basis, yet she hated the idea of never seeing him at all.

Sounds of laughter and music began to intrude on her dark thoughts as they approached the festivities. Security lights lit the park area while colored lanterns adorned the shelter house. The concrete skating rink had been cleared for dancing, and the evening phase of the celebration was well underway.

Katlyn quickened her pace, but Jared wasn't ready to let her slip away from him entirely. He leaned down and put his mouth close to her ear. "I think you're wrong about us, and I plan to change your mind," he promised softly.

A shiver raced down her spine. "I have to use the bathroom," she insisted, stepping out of his reach, then making a beeline for the ladies' rest room, where Jared couldn't follow.

Splashing cold water on her face helped a little. She felt as if she'd run a marathon. She'd definitely run a gauntlet of emotions in the past hour. Resisting her attraction to Jared was a whole lot easier when they were apart. Doing it when and if he followed through with his vow to change her mind would be quite a challenge.

She swept a comb through her hair and smoothed it back into its usual sleek style. It was naturally straight except for the ends that curled under slightly. Fortunately, the heavy texture didn't easily tangle.

Jared's hands had wreaked havoc, but Katlyn quickly repaired the damage. She wished she could repair the damage to her heart as easily.

Now what? she wondered, staring at herself in the

aging mirror above the sink. How could she go back out and join the party feeling as fragile as she did right now?

She was tempted to sneak home, but that would be a real show of cowardice. Ryan would know she was upset and come looking for her. Aunt Trudy probably would, too, and she didn't want to ruin their evenings.

Would Jared care if she left? Did she want him to? No. She had to get on with her life and that meant learning to socialize with the same people he did. As long as he didn't make a scene, she could cope.

A couple of teenage girls entered the rest room, spurring Katlyn into action. She tucked the comb into her back pocket, gave them a brief greeting, and moved out the door. Then she walked through the shelter house and headed for the crowd milling around the dance floor.

A band of local musicians was playing music for a country line dance, and several groups of dancers were already taking part in the fun. Normally Katlyn loved dancing, but she didn't feel like it right now.

Her aunt, Trudy, and some friends had moved their lawn chairs to the grassy area near the floor to watch the dancers. It was an annual ritual for most of them. Their feet were as busy keeping time to the music as their mouths were trying to talk loud enough to be heard over it.

Katlyn mustered a smile as she took a seat by her aunt and nodded to her friends. She knew they all thought of her as a fallen woman. It didn't bother her as much as annoy her. No one really had the right to pass judgment on her, of course, but some people did anyway. She just hoped Trudy's friends didn't upset her aunt with their opinions.

Aunt Trudy patted her leg affectionately and leaned close enough to be heard. "Ryan was looking for you. He needed a partner," she said.

Katlyn nodded, then scanned the floor for Ryan. He was never really short of partners. There were plenty of willing women vying for his time and attention. Mostly he used her to ward them off, but she understood and didn't mind at all. There were probably people who thought they were lovers, too, so now the gossips' tongues should really be flapping.

Her gaze involuntarily searched the crowds for Jared. He wasn't dancing, but she caught sight of him on the opposite side of the floor. When she shifted her eyes to his face, their gazes locked, and sparks flew. Katlyn quickly switched her attention back to Trudy.

"Why aren't you out there?" she asked.

"I'm too old for those fancy new dances," argued her aunt.

At fifty-eight, Trudy wasn't too old for anything. She was trim, attractive and energetic. The Vietnam war had made her a young widow. She'd never shown an interest in remarrying, but there were plenty of suitors. Her biggest concern stemmed from not wanting to show any of them preferential treatment.

"You're not old," Katlyn argued absently as the lively tune ended and a slower one started.

Ryan was beside her and asking her to dance in less than a minute. She knew he was concerned about her, so she accepted his hand and allowed

him to draw her into the growing crunch of dancers. She slid into his arms with the ease of famili-
arity, then watched as other couples joined them on
the floor.

At the sight of sexy, single, Mary Jo Connors coax-
ing Jared to dance, she swiftly brought her gaze
back to Ryan's watchful eyes.

"Well?" he prompted.

"Well, what?" she hedged.

"Well, hell, I don't know," he grumbled. "Who's
been occupying your every thought for weeks now?"

Katlyn wrinkled her nose at him. "*Who* is dancing
with Mary Jo."

"She's on the prowl tonight," Ryan explained un-
necessarily. "I'm seriously thinking of taking her up
on the offer if she doesn't manage to lasso King
first."

Katlyn's brows furrowed in a frown, but her dis-
taste for the idea dug even deeper. A white-hot jolt
of jealousy stung her at the thought of Jared with
another woman.

"You can't have it both ways, darlin'," Ryan reminded.

She scowled at him. "I know."

"But you don't like it?"

"Not even a tiny bit," replied Katlyn. She decided
to keep her gaze glued to Ryan so it wouldn't stray
to where Mary Jo was practicing really loud body
language on Jared.

Ryan returned her gaze with steady intensity.
"Think he'll take the bait?"

Katlyn's breath hitched, her heart aching at the
suggestion. She hoped not. She couldn't bear the
thought of Jared with another woman. The idea

made her physically ill, even though she knew she had no rightful claim on his loyalty.

When she had her unruly emotions in check again, she managed a lighthearted response. "This love stuff is hell, isn't it?"

"Yeah, I'll second that."

Katlyn searched his handsome features, unable to voice the question hovering on her mind.

Ryan answered the unspoken query. "No, it's not the same," he assured her. "If you and I had ever been lovers, it might be different."

His comments prompted a blush and a little laughter. "See, I always told you it would be a mistake to become physically involved," she teased.

"Well . . ." His tone turned wicked, his eyes devilish. "I'd be willing to trade some suffering for a long night of wild, uninhibited sex right now."

Katlyn laughed at his teasing. They'd always shared an earthy rapport, and very few subjects were taboo between them.

"In that case, you'd better go pry Mary Jo from Jared. She's your best hope tonight."

Ryan glanced toward the other couple. "She does have a body to die for," he mumbled.

"Only because you have a preference for busty women."

"That I do," he admitted with a rakish grin.

Katlyn grinned back at him as the music came to an end and the band took a short break. She urged Ryan to find a more enthusiastic partner while she returned to her seat next to Trudy. She gladly accepted a cold soft drink from her aunt and drank thirstily.

Jared separated himself from Mary Jo as they left

the floor, easing Katlyn's mind a bit. She chastised herself for watching his every move, yet her gaze followed him as he joined a group of other ranchers.

His easy camaraderie with the older generation reminded her of the first time they'd met. They'd both been visiting Judd Harmon at the county hospital. Judd, a long-time employee of the Kings and a long-time customer of Aunt Trudy's, had just been diagnosed with terminal cancer.

With no blood relatives and no savings, the wiry old cowboy was petrified of becoming a ward of the state. Jared had assured him that the Kings took care of their own. He'd proven his loyalty by having Judd, along with a private nurse, transferred to the King homestead for his final weeks of life.

It was during those weeks that Katlyn had lost her heart. She'd visited as often as possible and witnessed the inherent kindness of the man beneath Jared King's cool, impassive facade.

His patience and compassion for his friend had earned her undying respect. He'd managed to assist the proud old cowboy while allowing Judd to retain as much dignity as possible.

The three of them had played cards, shared silly jokes and laughed at anecdotes from Judd's life on the ranch. The time seemed to have passed in a heartbeat, yet Katlyn's world was forever altered. Her burgeoning admiration for Jared, coupled with their fierce physical attraction, had tossed her haplessly into an ill-fated love affair.

A rousing tune interrupted Katlyn's reverie, and she realized the band's break was over. Another friend invited her to dance, and the bittersweet memories were shoved aside. A steady stream of partners kept her busy for the next few hours. She put aside her personal problems to enjoy a rare evening of socializing. Before long, the band was announcing their final song.

As she started to return to her seat, Jared suddenly appeared at her side, pulling her gently into his arms. A whimper of protest died on Katlyn's lips as she gazed into his dark eyes. For just an instant his expression seemed imploring and needy. It made her heartbeat falter, so she yielded herself to his embrace.

She was hot and tired and willing to lean into his strength. He pulled her intimately close, wrapping his arms around her waist, the action compelling her to slide her hands over his chest.

He was big and warm and solid, the feel of him familiar and arousing. The soft curves of her body adjusted to the hard shape of his; male to female with electrifying results.

Katlyn was at a loss to control her physical responses. Jared's seductive caresses earlier in the evening had left her nerves alive with anticipation. She attempted to dispel the feelings with light banter.

"We really will have the gossips confused tonight," she suggested, trapping his gaze with her own. "They were so sure you'd dumped me, and now they'll be all the more curious."

The fire in his eyes was hot and possessive, caressing her as seductively as his body. She couldn't suppress a quiver of reaction.

"I don't give a damn what they think."

Katlyn knew he spoke the truth. She wished she could be as independent. Life would be a whole lot simpler, and she wouldn't feel so torn by years of being a good girl, who always did what was expected of her.

For the next few minutes, they swayed gently to the pulsing beat of the ballad being played, partially hidden in the shadows. Jared's fingers flexed on her hips, then moved up her rib cage and along her arms.

He grasped her hands and pulled them over his shoulders to wrap around his neck, then slowly slid his hands back down her arms. His thumbs brushed the sides of her breasts in an intimate caress that left Katlyn trembling.

Once his hands were cupping her hips again, he pulled her still closer, showing her how much the feel of her aroused him. Her breath shattered and blood pounded heavily through her veins.

"Come home with me," he whispered gruffly, nuzzling her neck with hot lips.

Katlyn closed her eyes against another threat of tears, and wrapped her arms more tightly about his neck. There was nothing she wanted more right now than to agree. Her body strained for closer contact with his, instinctively seeking the satisfaction it knew he could give.

She ached, and knew that he ached, too.

"I can't, Jared," she whispered back to him. "Because I won't stay, and I can't bear to leave again."

Three

Jared dragged himself out of bed and took a cold shower. Another night of restless sleep wasn't going to be made better by the pounding of the spray, but he hoped it might shock his system into alertness.

He had hundreds of young calves to separate from their mothers today, a dozen men to supervise and work that demanded his undivided attention.

Damn Katlyn. He damned her regularly for being a dream lover who taunted him day and night. He damned her for being childishly sweet and stripper sexy; innocent, yet provocative. He damned her for relentlessly occupying his thoughts and for walking out on him after giving him weeks of sensual pleasure that had no equal.

He'd thought she'd come back if he didn't chase after her. He'd been wrong. She'd meant it when she'd said goodbye. He'd thought he could convince her to come home if he tried, but she'd stood her ground. He'd been wrong again.

She didn't just want him—she wanted the King name. He'd thought she was different from all the rest, and he didn't like being wrong. In fact, it made him furious and ate at him like a disease.

He'd learned early in life that he couldn't trust anyone but himself. That lesson had been ham-

mered into him constantly over the years. First by
his grandfather, then his parents with their assorted
spouses, and by the few women he'd allowed himself to trust.

Everybody wanted a piece of what he had. But
the ranch and his land were his life, his heritage,
his future . . . and they were his heart and soul.
He'd be damned if he'd part with any of it.

A hearty breakfast and a pot full of strong coffee
helped take the edge off his irritability before he
headed to the barns. The men had been grumbling
about his bad temper, and he was determined to
keep a tight lid on it. He was tired of their specu-
lations about his love life and he wanted it to stop.

He hadn't intended for Katlyn to become involved with the workings of the ranch while she'd
been living with him. He'd wanted to protect her
from crude comments, speculation and ogling. By
keeping her a virtual prisoner in the house, he'd
hoped to spare her. All he'd accomplished was to
pique his men's interest and alienate her.

" 'Morning, boss."

" 'Morning, Dan." Jared greeted his foreman just
outside the back door and fell into step with him.
They strode toward the main barn where the men
would be awaiting daily orders.

"I think I'd better warn you that the guys are all
stirred up this morning," said Dan, a middle-aged
cowboy whose job as foreman sometimes included
mediation.

"What's up?"

"Eli Carson was in town yesterday and overheard
a heated conversation between Miss Katlyn and old
lady Pearson at the hardware store."

"Dora Pearson is a meddling old busybody," insisted Jared. His tone was dismissive, but he braced himself for any discussion concerning Katlyn.

"I know, I know," Dan agreed. "She spreads her venom to anybody she can hold hostage at the cash register, but I thought you'd want to hear about this one."

"What's she up to now?"

"Well," Dan hesitated as if choosing his words with care. "It seems the old gal was telling one of her cronies that you had the morals of a tomcat. She was goin' on about how you corrupted poor Katlyn, used her until you'd had your fill, then tossed her aside like so much baggage."

Jared stopped abruptly at the entrance to the barn, muttered a few choice obscenities and leveled black eyes on his foreman.

Dan threw up his hands as if to ward off his ire. "I know, I know, there's not a grain of truth in it, but you know how sanctimonious an old woman like that can be."

"Katlyn heard all of it?"

Dan nodded his balding head. "Sure enough. She took in every word and then set Dora straight. Eli said Katlyn told her and everyone in the store that she'd come to live with you by her own choice and left the same way. Then she said that her personal life was nobody's business, and they should worry about mindin' their own for a change."

Jared's protective instincts warred with amusement and pride. He hated that Katlyn had had to defend herself, but was pleased and proud that she'd done it. As long as she was a slave to public opinion, she'd never have a life of her own.

"I suppose Eli's been rehashing the story to all the men." Eli was the ranch's version of the town crier.

"Yep. He especially likes the part where Katlyn told old lady Pearson she'd better never hear her bad-mouthin' you again, 'cause those who cast the first stone usually get beat to death."

Dan chuckled at the retelling.

Jared groaned, his gut twisting. Katlyn was under siege and it was his fault. When he'd asked her to move in with him, he'd never given a thought to all the busybodies in town. Now she was warring with everyone who dared criticize him.

"That little lady has spunk. Mary says Katlyn's a sweetheart unless she's riled. I reckon old Pearson must have riled her good."

Mary Welder, Dan's wife of twenty years, was one of the few women Jared trusted and admired. Although she always knew what was happening in Kingston, she never repeated malicious gossip nor tried to impose her beliefs on others.

"Katlyn thinks Mary's a sweetheart, too." Jared surprised himself by sharing. He rarely spoke of her to anyone, and even less rarely stated her opinion. He wanted emotional distance, but thoughts of her kept sneaking past his defenses.

"Mary's the best," boasted Dan. "Of course, she can also be bullheaded and contrary, but don't go tellin' her I said so."

Jared threw Dan a knowing look and entered the barn ahead of him, then continued through the building toward the tack room where the men would be assembled. As they drew closer, snatches of conversation could be heard. He heard Katlyn's name mentioned and his mood darkened.

The room went silent when he and Dan entered. A few greetings were exchanged, and then Jared wasted no time putting a stop to speculation.

"I'm going to say this once and that's the end of it," he told them grimly. "I hate gossip, whether it's from mean-spirited old women or well-intentioned ranch hands."

His remark prompted a chorus of grumbling.

"A man's gotta stay informed," dared one young hand.

"There ain't no comparison," muttered another. "Women gossip, men just tell it like it is."

Yet another said, "We were just relatin' the truth."

"But, boss," Eli argued with a cocky tone and smile. "Your lady was awesome."

Jared's jaws clenched in frustration. He knew Katlyn was awesome. He also knew they were all dying of curiosity. They wanted to know the details. Why Katlyn had left him. How he intended to handle the situation. Whether or not she was still his woman.

Most of his staff had seen them together at the festival and wondered, like the rest of the community, where their relationship stood. Hell, *he* didn't even know. The thought hardened his tone. "My private life is just that. Private. I don't interfere in yours, so keep your noses out of mine."

More grumbling accompanied his order, but it was good-natured grumbling. As one of the best employers in the area, he was a fair, hard-working boss, and he'd earned their respect years ago.

"One more thing before we get to work," he added, pinning Eli, the leader of the pack, with a piercing gaze. "Katlyn is no longer a topic of bunk-house discussion. If she's ever in need of help, I'd expect each of you to back her up, but that doesn't give you the right to speculate about her private life."

"Are you sayin' she's still your woman, and we should watch out for her?" taunted the younger men.

His persistence was making Jared angrier by the minute, but he reined in his temper. "I'm saying this discussion is at an end," he snapped.

"Time to get to work," Dan added judiciously. "We need to split into two crews today."

Jared stood back and let Dan organize the men. As usual, the foreman would accompany one crew while he supervised the other. Ironically, they'd all wanted to work with him while Katlyn was in residence. Now they all vied to be on Dan's crew.

He didn't think his temperament changed so drastically, but his foreman assured him it had. If he suffered some physical withdrawal from her heated attentions, that was only to be expected.

Katlyn had spoiled him and now she was defending him in public. He didn't want her fighting battles over him. He was tired of their relationship being fodder for gossip, but he knew it was his own fault.

Asking her to move in with him had been a mistake. A costly one for his peace of mind. Still, despite all the arguments against the arrangement, he wanted her back. He'd just have to change tactics.

He considered several options over the course of

the day. The young calves didn't like being separated from their cows, but most of the process was handled without problems. The men did their usual complaining, though.

By quitting time, Jared was hot, tired and hungry, yet satisfied with the day's work. The afternoon sun dipped into the horizon as he and Dan walked toward the foreman's truck.

"Mary says you're welcome to join us for supper," said Dan.

"Tell her thanks, but I think I'm going to Trudy's Café for supper."

The older man's eyes widened. "I didn't know you patronized Trudy's."

"Haven't been there for a few years, but I hear they've remodeled and serve a good meal."

"Yeah, the place is real nice now," the foreman agreed in a carefully neutral tone. "And the new cook really knows her stuff."

"Chef," Jared corrected automatically. "That's the proper title for someone who's gone to one of those fancy cooking schools."

"Well, I sure wanna be politically correct," insisted Dan. "Now mind you don't get into any trouble. I don't want to hafta come bail you out of jail for disturbin' the peace," he added as he climbed into his truck.

"I'm not looking for trouble."

"Just mendin' fences?"

Jared ignored the question. "Tell Mary thanks for the invitation. I'll take a rain check."

"Will do," promised Dan as he slammed the truck door and revved the engine to life.

Jared watched as he exited the drive and turned

down the road toward his own home. In a few minutes, his foreman would be welcomed by Mary and their three kids. They'd converge on Dan as soon as he walked in the door. He'd grumble about fielding the barrage of questions, but he'd love every minute of the attention.

Jared quickly stifled a pang of envy and strode toward his own empty house. He braced himself for the quiet as he entered, cursing Katlyn as he did so. Until she'd come and gone, the solitude hadn't bothered him. Most days, he'd welcomed it.

Now he missed the mouth-watering aromas that had greeted him while she was here. He missed the hugs and kisses, her delighted, welcoming smiles and husky laughter. He missed the way his whole body had come alive with excitement whenever she was near.

He also resented the fact that he missed her so much; that he ached for her in ways that were uncharacteristic and disturbing. He refused to analyze all the reasons he missed her, but he was determined to get her back on his own terms.

With that thought, he swiftly showered and changed clothes. Less than an hour after saying goodbye to Dan, Jared pulled his truck to a stop in the parking lot of Trudy's Café. He surveyed the renovated building with an appreciative eye.

As a boy, his grandpa had brought him to Trudy's once in a while. Back then, the diner had been housed in a converted garage attached to Trudy Sanders's big old two-story house. A year ago, she'd totally remodeled a small barn on the property and moved the restaurant there.

The interior of the building was another surprise.

The renovations had enhanced the rustic quality of the high-beamed ceilings and loft. The country decor was bright and colorful. Tables were covered with checkered tablecloths in a variety of colors. In the center of each was a fat, flickering candle.

The old soda fountain and counter with stools still graced one wall, with a dozen or so tables scattered around the bottom floor of the building. There were more tables in the loft, but that area was dark.

The restaurant closed at eight, and it was already half past seven. There were only a few patrons seated at tables and a couple on stools at the counter.

"Good evening, Mr. King." He was greeted by a teenage hostess who gave him a bright, nervous smile. "Would you like to be seated or are you here to join someone?"

"I'm alone, and I'd like a seat near the kitchen," he told her, smiling slightly as her eyes went wide with surprise.

He followed her to the center of the room, to a table near the swinging doors that led to the kitchen. He laid his hat on one chair and sat in another, but refused the offer of a menu.

"I know it's late. I'll eat whatever's left. Katlyn knows what I like. Just tell her I'm starving."

"Yes, sir."

She went to the kitchen, and returned shortly with a tall glass of iced tea and a fresh salad. In a few more minutes, she returned with a steaming bowl of beef stew and a plate of biscuits dripping with butter. His mouth watered, and he wasted no time satisfying his hunger.

While he ate, he watched the staff slowly go about their closing chores without seeming to rush the customers. A couple of people greeted him as they headed toward the counter where Trudy operated the cash register.

At closing time, when he was the only customer left, she approached his table. They greeted each other with wary politeness.

Instead of throwing him out on his ear as he half-expected, she only asked, "Can I get you some dessert, Jared?"

Her congeniality was a welcome surprise. He pushed his empty dishes aside and smiled self–consciously. "I don't think I've got room."

Trudy's eyes twinkled. "Katlyn baked fresh apple pies this evening. How about an à la mode?"

Jared moaned a little and grinned. He loved Katlyn's apple pie. "Maybe just a small piece without the ice cream."

She nodded, gathered his dirty dishes and went to the kitchen, leaving him to wonder about her attitude. They'd never gotten to know each other, but he knew the older woman resented the fact that he'd invited Katlyn to move in with him.

Maybe she wasn't upset about it anymore now that Katlyn was back. It was hard to tell if he'd just been offered an olive branch or if she was only extending him professional hospitality.

The pie melted in his mouth, and he savored every bite. While he ate, the staff departed one by one until Trudy was the only one left in the dining room. When she began to count the cash in the register, he moved toward the counter, reaching for his wallet.

"Your dinner is on the house," Trudy insisted.

Jared frowned. He didn't expect them to accommodate him at the last minute and then refuse payment.

"Take it up with Katlyn." Trudy held up her hand to forestall an argument. "She says you eat free here, anytime. Chefs of her caliber can be pretty temperamental, so I don't argue with her. You're welcome to try."

Her words accompanied a nod toward the kitchen door. Jared took it for tacit permission to trespass into Katlyn's private territory. He tossed down a couple of bills for the waitress's tip, then moved to the swinging doors.

Upon entering the long, narrow kitchen, he leaned against the doorjamb, crossed his arms over his chest and watched her at work. Katlyn was alone and seemed to be putting away the last of the food.

Dressed all in white, she had her hair pulled on top of her head and covered with some sort of net. Her cheeks were flushed a rosy pink, making her look incredibly innocent and appealing. Heat curled through his belly.

She didn't immediately see him. When she did, her eyes lit with pleasure, and the pleasure thrilled him more than he cared to consider. Then her lashes dropped to conceal her expression.

"Hello, Jared."

As always, the sultry sound of her voice warmed his blood and created a yearning within him that he couldn't quite define.

"Thanks for dinner. I know I came in late, but everything sure hit the spot."

He watched, fascinated, as her blush deepened.

He'd decided long ago that she was an intriguing mixture of shyness and siren.

"You're welcome," she said, as she untied her apron and tossed it in a laundry bin.

"How come you're not wearing one of those floppy chef's hats?" he asked.

Katlyn gave him a small smile. "The sad truth is they give me a headache. I don't like wearing them," she admitted. "Wearing a hair net is bad enough, but a real necessity in the business."

"I don't suppose customers appreciate hair in their food."

"No, and the Board of Health frowns on it, too," she added, busily rearranging utensils on the long, stainless-steel sink.

He was making her nervous. The realization took Jared by surprise. She wasn't the type to fidget, but she seemed uncomfortable with him. He didn't like it. They'd been as intimate as two people could be, yet she was treating him like an unexpected stranger.

He moved toward her and grasped her hand to still the nervous movements. A familiar heat coursed through him, but Katlyn stiffened, which annoyed him more. She finally lifted her head and looked directly into his eyes.

"Why are you here, Jared?"

"I was hungry . . . and tired of my own cooking."

She searched his face. "That's it?"

He shook his head briefly in denial, his gaze never leaving hers. "You know that's not it. I haven't changed my mind about anything. If you won't come to me, then I'll come to you until you decide to move back home."

She glanced down at his hand on her wrist, but she didn't shake free of his grasp. Encouraged, he began to stroke his thumb slowly over the soft flesh. He was rewarded by the leap in her pulse. His own leapt in response.

"I haven't changed my mind about anything, either," she insisted quietly.

"You don't miss me?" he asked, then cleared the sudden huskiness from his voice.

Katlyn dropped her gaze again. "I never said I didn't miss you."

"Then why fight what you feel? Do you think it's a sin to enjoy being together? Do you know how many people wish they have what we have?"

Katlyn pulled from his grip. "All we *had* was physical attraction."

Jared let the comment pass as his gaze roamed over her face; the high cheekbones, wide set eyes and generous mouth. He'd met women with more classically beautiful features, but never one who captivated him as much. Never one who enticed him just by breathing.

He didn't quite understand the depth of his attraction to her, but he wanted to explore it further. He wanted Katlyn back—in his home, his bed, his life.

Stunned, he realized that he'd settle for a kiss or touch or any freely offered intimacy right at the moment. He badly wanted some sign that she needed him as much as he needed her; some evidence that she was sorry she'd left him.

"Katlyn." Trudy called to her from the dining room. "I'm heading home. I'll lock up out here."

"I'm right behind you," she called back, then said to him, "I'm ready to call it a night."

"I'll help you lock up."

"That's not necessary."

Jared didn't argue, he just moved through the kitchen with her as she shut off lights and locked the back door. Once outside, he tested the doorknob and turned to Katlyn again. She tried to say good night, but he insisted on walking her home. They fell into step together.

A small brick path led from the restaurant's parking lot to Trudy's house The area was well lit even though the night was pitch dark. There was a nip in the air, but it was refreshing after the warmth of the kitchen.

"Converting the barn to a restaurant was a great idea. Trudy's made it into a nice place."

"We're really proud of it," said Katlyn.

"What made her decide to expand?"

"Finances, mostly," she explained. "My aunt saved for years to make sure I could have the best education possible. She wanted me to attend a four-year college, but I just didn't want to. We compromised. I went to culinary school, she invested the rest of the money in the restaurant, and we formed a partnership."

Jared frowned at the disclosure. He hadn't known Katlyn was so deeply involved in her aunt's business, although he knew she loved to cook. She'd cooked for him, so he hadn't thought about her missing the restaurant. Nor had he considered the problems that must have created for the business.

"Who did the cooking while you lived with me?"

He'd convinced her to take some time off during that month.

"Aunt Trudy cooks when necessary, and we have two other ladies who help. They were both happy to pick up extra hours. I also arranged for a couple of apprentice chefs from my school to work. We were satisfied that the quality of cooking never suffered, and we didn't have any complaints."

Jared digested the new information; the side of Katlyn he'd never explored. They'd reached Trudy's porch, and he followed her up the steps. At the door, she turned and faced him, her body language saying goodbye before she voiced the words.

"Do you have to call it a night or would you like to take a ride? We can drive around for a while and listen to some music." There was little else to do this time of night in Kingston.

She hesitated, but her refusal was firm when she spoke. "Thanks, but I'm really tired. One of the other cooks called in sick this afternoon, so I've had a long day."

"You have to work tomorrow, too?"

"Just in the evening."

He studied her face in the soft light. She'd pulled the net off her hair and shaken it free of confinement. The heavy locks made a dark, satiny frame for her lovely features. He curled his fingers into fists to keep from sinking them into the familiar softness.

"Are you always responsible for handling staff shortages?"

"Aunt Trudy and I share the duties. We aren't at the stage where we can sit back and rake in profits. Sometimes we have to work a lot of hours, but it's beginning to pay off in terms of our reputation and financial security."

Jared considered her hard-working, common sense approach to the business. It had always been the same for him at the ranch, but he wondered why they'd never discussed it before now.

"How come you never told me any of this?" he demanded.

Katlyn took a small step to close the distance between them. Without touching him anywhere else, she rose on tiptoe and placed a brief, tantalizing kiss on his lips.

"Because you never asked," she said softly.

He stared at the door for a few minutes after she'd closed it in his face. Uncurling his fingers, he lifted them to his lips, wondering why the feel of that tiny kiss shot through him like a bolt of lightning.

Why had his interest in her work been worthy of a kiss when nothing else he'd offered seemed to make an impression? He shook his head in confusion. Women! How was a man supposed to know what mattered most to them? In his experience, only money and social status made a lasting impression.

He still couldn't figure Katlyn's angle. Was marriage the only real interest she had in him? Was she hoping that his name would help her business interests as well? What better way to make an impression in Kingston than with the King name?

Following that thought came the question of how their living together had impacted the business at Trudy's Café. He'd be willing to bet their profits had doubled from customers wanting the latest gossip as well as food.

It had been the same all his life. Someone always expected financial gain from any relationship with a King. His heart told him Katlyn was different, but his head wasn't totally convinced.

Four

For the next three evenings, Katlyn caught herself glancing frequently toward the dining room when she worked, but Jared didn't come again. She brutally crushed the hope that had blossomed after his initial visit.

On Saturday, business was especially busy, so there was little time to think about anything but cooking. Closing time on the weekends was the same, but people tended to come in later and stay longer.

Jared was no exception. It was almost eight o'clock when he arrived and ordered his dinner. The rest of her staff had gone and it was nearing nine when he finally made his way to the kitchen.

Katlyn was both pleased and annoyed. Her heart leapt with pleasure at the sight of him, yet her confidence was shaken. She was hot, disheveled and stressed. He was cool, calm and, as always, in control.

"Hello, Katlyn."

The deep, masculine sound of his voice made her pulse flutter. Dressed in jeans and a pale blue cotton shirt, he was all hard, virile male. His steady, scrutinizing gaze rested on her face, and she felt the familiar warmth his presence always produced.

She greeted him as she washed her hands one final time. "Hi, Jared. How was your dinner?"

He crossed his arms over his chest and leaned a shoulder against the door frame. "It was fine, thanks."

Katlyn dried her hands, dropped the towel in the hamper and reached for some hand lotion. She slowly approached him as she rubbed the cream over her hands.

"If you'd come a little earlier, you might actually get to choose your own meal instead of settling for leftovers."

He cocked a brow at her scolding. "I'm not picky. Even your leftovers are better than frozen dinners."

"Thanks, I guess," she said. Then she tugged the net from her hair and gently shook her head, sighing with relief.

Jared's gaze followed her every move, making her intensely aware of his scrutiny. She knew she looked like something the cat dragged in. Having always tried to look her best for him, she wondered what he thought of the real, totally unglamorous Katlyn.

"Trudy wouldn't let me pay for my meal again tonight. I'm not a charity case, you know. Money might be tight, but I can still afford the basics."

Her gaze searched his rugged features. She wondered if the gesture had wounded his pride, not that she really cared. He wouldn't suffer any real damage, and turnabout was fair play.

"Are you complaining?" she asked, propping her hands on her hips.

"Yeah, I expect to pay for my food the next time I come in."

"Forget it. I didn't pay room and board when I

lived with you, so I don't plan to let you pay for anything when you're at my place."

"Do you think I was running a tab for you?" he countered. "How long before we're even? If you want to get technical, I'll have to pay your chef's fees for all that free cooking you did at my place."

"Why don't we agree that friends don't pay at friends' houses?" she suggested lightly.

Jared's expression grew serious. "Are we friends, Katlyn?"

She frowned a little and gave the concept some thought. "I think we could be," she said, "but we really don't know each other very well, do we?"

He took his time responding. "Why don't you think we know each other? We've been as close as two people can be. I know you have a birthmark on the top of your left thigh. I know your ribs are ticklish. I know the scent and taste and feel of you. Doesn't that count for anything?"

The sexy, intimate tone of his voice sent delicious chills down Katlyn's spine, but she resisted the pull of attraction. She needed to clear the air between them. If Jared was really interested in renewing their relationship, there were issues they needed to address.

"Do you know what my favorite color is? My favorite flower? Who my other friends are? How important my work is to me? What books I like to read? What makes me happy or sad?"

His eyes narrowed. "It takes time to get to know somebody that way. You didn't give us a whole lot of time, did you?"

"Or maybe we started the process backwards,"

she said, hating the warmth she felt creeping over her neck and cheeks.

"Meaning?" he drawled.

"Meaning people usually get to know each other over a period of time, become friends, then lovers."

"And you think we went about it the wrong way 'round?"

Katlyn's stance became more stiff and defensive. "Yes. If all you want is for me to be your roommate and lover, then you're wasting your time. I'm not going to change my mind."

Her blush deepened as she issued the challenge. It wasn't easy for her to talk about their private life, but it was crucial to her emotional well-being. He had to decide if he wanted more than a body to warm his bed.

"You don't want to be lovers?" he asked.

Jared's low, gruff tone stirred memories of endless nights in his arms, and of his amazing, unselfish passion. A different kind of warmth invaded her veins.

"I want to be friends first," she insisted softly, fighting the physical pull on her senses.

"You want a courtship?"

Her eyes widened at his use of the old-fashioned term. She stared at him for a while before responding. The concept was thrilling at one level, yet worrisome on another. She really wanted the chance to know him better, but what if he didn't like her very much once he *had* gotten to know her? If they got to know each other, would it kill the excitement and dampen his interest? It was a risk worth taking.

Her words were slow in coming. "Yes. Yes, I guess maybe that is what I want."

"Then how about a date?" asked Jared. "We could catch a late movie or go listen to some music."

The invitation secretly thrilled her, but she gave him a cheeky grin. "Sorry, I already have plans for the evening."

Jared's relaxed stance stiffened immediately. He uncrossed his arms and straightened. "You have a date?"

"A poker date," she teased.

"Poker?"

"Trudy has a friendly little poker club that meets here every Saturday night after closing. I promised to play tonight."

Katlyn watched some of the tension drain from his body. She could tell Jared was trying to come to terms with the idea of Trudy playing poker. His image of her aunt was all straightlaced and morally uptight.

"Is this a high-stakes game?" he asked.

"Five dollar maximum."

"Does the sheriff know you're running an illegal gambling operation?"

"Sure. We deal him in every other Saturday when he's off duty."

"Illegal gambling, and conspiracy to bribe an officer of the law. Trudy must like living on the wild side," he taunted.

"No doubt about it. Want us to cut you in for some of the action?"

He seemed surprised by the offer, and Katlyn smiled wider. She knew he wasn't used to impromptu invitations, and he wasn't much of a team player. But he could learn.

"I guess I could handle five bucks. Especially since I didn't have to pay for my dinner."

"Trudy supplies the snacks, too."

"Sounds like a bargain. What needs to be done before we start?"

"I'm finished in here except for locking doors and turning out lights," she explained.

He helped with those small chores, then they moved into the dining room where Trudy was setting up for the game.

"Aunt Trudy, we have to deal Jared in this evening. If not, he might report our illegal operation to the local authorities."

"His money's as good as any other," her aunt replied, throwing them a smile.

"I'm going to get out of these work clothes. Jared, make yourself useful."

Jared nodded, and Trudy drummed out some instructions. They shifted tables and chairs to make one large table that would seat at least six card players.

In the bathroom, Katlyn exchanged her white uniform for jeans and a clean yellow T-shirt. She bathed her face, applied some perfume and makeup, then brushed her hair. It was a little kinky from being pinned up all evening, but there wasn't much she could do about that.

Excitement curled in her stomach. Just being near Jared did that to her. It was probably a mistake to hold onto the fragile hope that he might learn to care for her in a deeper sense, but she couldn't seem to obliterate it entirely.

She reentered the dining room just as Trudy was greeting Ryan Havens. Katlyn flinched, having forgotten that he sometimes showed up at their poker games. It was hard to tell how he and Jared would interact. They shared their usual stilted hellos.

Greetings were exchanged, and a few introductions made. Trudy's best friend, Eva, a lively redhead, was a regular. As a lifelong Kingston resident, she knew everyone.

Diminutive, white-haired Donna, the sixth member of their party, was one of their newest waitresses and a newcomer to town. She was joining them for the first time, but she wasn't the least bit shy. She introduced herself as a bored retiree who was always on the lookout for a good time.

Trudy and Eva sat down at one end of the table while Katlyn sat at the other end. Ryan took a seat to her right and Donna was on her left. Jared sat to Donna's left, so that he was opposite Katlyn.

Everyone bought a hundred poker chips for five dollars, so that each had an equal stake to begin the game.

"What are we playing?" asked Jared.

"Dealer's choice," explained Katlyn. "With Trudy, it's always five card stud."

"That's right," her aunt said as she began to shuffle the cards. "Ante up!"

For the next hour, they shared a lot of good-natured teasing and some pretty awful jokes. There was laughter, grumbling and shifting of poker chips.

Katlyn tried to concentrate on her cards, but it was hard with Jared so close. His steady gaze was riveted on her most of the time, and she was nervous for both of them. She badly wanted him to enjoy himself. It was so rare for him to take time to play. It pleased her that he was making an effort to relax and socialize with her friends.

Ryan was unusually quiet. He made a few teasing remarks to her that caused Jared's mouth to tighten, but Katlyn imagined she was the only one who noticed the extra bit of tension.

Another hour into the game and Jared had lost nearly all his chips. "Can I buy more?" he asked.

Katlyn answered, "Nope, you can borrow some, but you can't buy more."

He glanced around the table and then back to her. "Looks like you're the only one with chips to spare. Want to float me a loan?"

"Sure, but the payback is two to one."

He raised his brows. "What! That's criminal," he accused. Then he glanced at Trudy for direction. "She allowed to get away with that?" he asked.

Katlyn struggled to keep a straight face. It tickled her that he appealed to Trudy for fairness. It was a small act of respect that meant a lot.

"She can be a real loan shark," the older woman admitted, shaking her head in mock regret. "I know it's unfair, but the player with the most chips sets the rules."

"Cutthroat, that's what I call it," Jared groused, his eyes challenging Katlyn to soften her demands. "I thought you said you were running a friendly little game here."

"Are you in or out, King?" She didn't give an inch and it was her deal. "The game is seven card, deuces wild. You want a loan or not?"

"I'll take twenty chips."

"That means you pay back forty or the equivalent in cash," she reminded.

"I can do the math, dealer. But you'd better hope you don't need a loan tonight."

His grumbling and spirited comeback delighted Katlyn, making her laugh out loud. Their gazes locked, and Jared smiled a wickedly pleased smile. The beauty of it made her breath hitch. When she realized that her laughter made him happy, too, her heart filled with quiet joy.

She momentarily forgot everything but him. Her hands stilled, and her gaze stayed locked with his in hypnotic fascination. He had the most incredible eyes, especially when they glittered with amusement.

Any woman could get lost in those dark, mysterious depths. He wasn't playful by nature, so it thrilled her when he relaxed enough to verbally spar with her. She'd missed him unbearably, so just having him close was a thrill in itself.

Ryan suddenly scraped his chair backward, snapping Katlyn out of her spellbound silence. Then everyone began to talk at once.

"Time for a break," said Trudy.

"I think I'd better visit the ladies' room," added Eva.

"I'll freshen our drinks," said Donna, rising and heading toward the soda fountain.

"I'm hungry for something sweet," said Ryan.

Realizing that the intimate exchange between her and Jared had provoked the sudden activity, Katlyn felt herself blushing. She forced her attention from him.

"You're always hungry for something sweet, Havens," she teased, flashing her friend an almost apologetic look. She hadn't meant to make him uncomfortable with her flirting. She hadn't meant to flirt at all, but her reactions to Jared were different than with any other man she'd ever known.

"You didn't happen to make turtle cheesecake today, did you?"

"Turtle cheesecake." Jared's interest was piqued. "I had dessert, but I could probably force down a piece of cheesecake."

Katlyn's head snapped back in his direction. "Force down?" she challenged.

"Uh-oh, you're in for a lecture," warned Ryan. "I think I'll go raid the fridge."

When the others had scattered, Jared rose and stretched; his broad chest and muscled arms straining the fabric of his shirt.

"Just teasing, Chef Sanders."

The sheer male gorgeousness of him combined with the rare, relaxed expression made her knees weak and her heart melt, but she didn't give him any slack.

"For your information, Mr. King, my culinary skills are not subject to teasing."

His eyes sparkled with wicked amusement. "Especially not when I'm trying to get you to float me a loan, huh?"

"Especially not then. The rate of exchange can be tripled or quadrupled," she warned.

"You're a hard woman, Katlyn Sanders," he insisted. His tone went deep with intimate challenge. "And you make some high demands."

Katlyn's heart did a little somersault. She knew his words had a double edge, but she didn't back down. Her voice dropped to a husky whisper.

"You'll be wise to remember that, Jared Alexander King."

Her use of his middle name dispelled the intimacy, brought forth a groan and had him shaking his head.

"I'd better complete this transaction before I get any deeper in debt," he insisted. "Give me twenty chips, and I'll pay back twice that amount."

"Providing you can win a hand or two." She shoved the chips across the table, then rose and stretched a little herself.

"I've just had a run of bad cards. I'll be ready to bail you out before the night's over."

"Yeah, right. That's what they all say."

The banter continued as everyone else returned to the table. Ryan brought cheesecake, and Donna brought a fresh round of drinks. Then they were back to poker.

It was well after midnight when they finally decided to call it quits. Jared had replenished his winnings. He'd repaid Katlyn and made a loan to Eva. Ryan had loaned money to Trudy that she didn't recoup, but he owed her from a previous game, so they called it even.

There were no real winners or losers. Except maybe for Katlyn, who'd enjoyed the pleasure of Jared's company for a few hours. Ryan volunteered to walk the other ladies to their cars. Jared and Katlyn agreed to lock up the restaurant.

She went to the kitchen and shut off the main light switches, then turned on the security light. When she returned to the dining room, the sound of music took her by surprise.

"I found the jukebox," Jared told her as he closed the distance between them.

The tune was one of her favorites; a slow, sexy

love song. The stirring sweetness of a popular saxophone melody enveloped them.

"Trudy couldn't bear to part with that old jukebox. But she said it didn't go well with our new look, so she buried it in a corner."

As she explained, he moved closer and slipped his arms around her. She stiffened briefly, her eyes searching his. They brooked no argument, but she didn't really want to argue. She'd been aching to touch him all night.

Lifting her hands to his chest, she luxuriated in the hard, warm, familiar feel of him. Silently warning herself not to get too comfortable, she eased more fully into his embrace. He felt so good.

He pulled her closer still, and she slid her hands around his neck. Resting her head near his shoulder, she noticed that the rhythmic beat of his heart was in time with the music, which mesmerized her.

The scent of his aftershave assaulted her senses and stirred up memories of untold intimacies. The solid strength of his body was a perfect counterpart to her softness. The steady brush of bodies reminded her of how perfectly they were attuned to each other.

She wanted him badly. Despite all her arguments for a platonic relationship, she couldn't deny the soul-deep longing to know his loving again. The need was impossible to deny, making her breasts swell and causing an ache deep within her.

He wanted her, too, and the hard evidence of that was firmly pressed against her. The physical desire hadn't diminished, but she wasn't fool enough to think anything else had changed.

His willingness to spend time with her was encouraging, but only an appetizer compared to the feast of attention she wanted and needed from him.

When the song ended, Katlyn slowly withdrew from his embrace. His eyes were deep, dark, seductive pools, and the hunger in them shook her composure. An unbearable tension pulsed between them.

"Come home with me," Jared insisted roughly. To strengthen his request, he slowly ran his hands up her sides, allowing his thumbs to brush her breasts before moving up to gently cup her face.

"I can't," she whispered before breaking eye contact.

"Why?" He sank his fingers into her hair and tilted her head up to his. "We both want it."

Katlyn fought the erotic sweetness of his touch. "I want a lot of things, but that doesn't mean they're all good for me," she replied in a broken whisper.

She felt him tense, and his fingers stilled.

"That's how you think about all this? Just something you think you should deny yourself? And you're a better person for not succumbing to temptation?"

A hint of temper invaded his tone. He still didn't understand her reluctance to be lovers, and she didn't know how else to explain.

"Maybe it doesn't make me a better person, but I can live with the decision."

With that, she eased from his touch and headed for the door. He followed more slowly. Once she'd closed and locked the restaurant, he walked her home. The night air was cool, the sky clear and bright with stars.

Jared didn't speak, but she sensed his resentment. What she couldn't judge was how much of that resentment was from physical frustration and how much from annoyance at not getting his own way.

She couldn't bear to end the night with hard feelings between them, so she reached out and grabbed his hand. He seemed surprised at first, then locked his fingers with hers.

"I'm glad you stayed tonight," she said as they reached the porch and faced each other.

Jared scrutinized her upturned face before quietly responding. "I enjoyed it."

"Did you?" she asked in a hopeful tone. She searched his features, too. "A penny ante poker game isn't exactly high-society entertainment."

"Nickel ante," he corrected quietly.

His teasing renewed the smile in Katlyn's eyes. "Cutthroat nickel ante."

"Cutthroat," he agreed, then reached out to brush a stray strand of hair from her cheek. He cupped the side of her face in his palm and stroked his thumb along her throat.

His touch sent thousands of tiny explosions through Katlyn. He seemed incapable of keeping his hands to himself, and the pleasure it continued to give her was intoxicating and addictive.

She closed her eyes and savored the feel of his big, warm hand on her skin. She missed his touch, his incredibly sensual touch. He'd taught her everything she knew about her own sensuality, and she desperately missed the way he could make her feel.

His grip tightened, and he slowly pulled her close enough to steal a kiss. It was barely a brush of his hard lips over hers, but it sent more tremors through her. She made a tiny, wanting sound and splayed her hands on his chest.

Jared brought his other hand up so that he was framing her face in his grip. With his hold on her, he controlled a series of slow, gentle kisses that left Katlyn wanting more.

She tried to deepen the kisses, but he wouldn't allow it. He held her at enough of a distance to prevent their lower bodies from seeking the satisfaction of contact. She mumbled her complaint against his mouth.

"Jared!"

"You can't have it both ways, Katlyn. I'm way past being satisfied with a few stolen caresses. What we had was too hot and sweet. You left me longing for you, and that's not going to change," he said softly, easing away from her.

Katlyn knew he was right, but she was trembling with frustration when she could no longer touch him. Her worst fear was that he'd satisfy his needs with someone else if she continued to refuse him. It seemed inevitable, but it tore her up to think about it.

"Anyway, thanks for dinner. And for dealing me in to your poker party."

"You're welcome." Breathless with desire, she could only watch as he turned and strode down the walk. She was tempted, so tempted, to follow.

Maybe we could still be lovers, she thought, feeling a rush of heat at the idea. She wouldn't have to move back in with him. They could just steal a few private hours now and then just like thousands of other couples. Would he be satisfied with such an arrangement? Would she? For how long?

Had she made unreasonable demands? Had she been unfair to expect him to change his attitude about marriage? Could he learn to trust her enough if she gave him more time? Or would he eventually tire of her and move on to someone more exciting, someone from his family's social circle?

They hadn't really known each other that long. Was she the biggest fool in the world for not taking every minute of time he was willing to give?

Katlyn didn't have the answers. All she could depend on was her own instincts, and instinct told her that Jared King would soon tire of any woman who let him have his own way too often.

Five

Katlyn spent the rest of the weekend debating whether or not to renew her love affair with Jared. He hadn't lost interest, as she'd feared, so the temptation hadn't lessened.

No matter how discreet they were, her aunt and everyone else in town would speculate. That didn't worry her as much as it initially had. At least not when compared to losing Jared for good. Since her reputation was already irreparably damaged, it just didn't seem so important anymore.

What really tore her apart was the idea of being Jared's mistress instead of his wife. Her biological clock was ticking. She desperately wanted a home of her own, children and the security of a future with the man she loved. Even more than that, she wanted him to love and respect her enough to offer all the rest. Would giving in to him cost her his respect in the long run? Or could she teach him to care enough?

The same questions had plagued her before her decision to leave Jared in the first place. Nothing much had changed except he'd proved his continued interest. If they became lovers again, it could be on her terms, part of the courtship ritual she badly wanted.

Sunday and Monday came and went without a word from Jared, making Katlyn doubt the wisdom of her newly formed decision.

By Tuesday morning, she acknowledged a major flaw in her plan. If they became lovers again, how could she handle only seeing him when he wanted sex? It would basically be the same as when she'd lived with him. Which put her right back to square one.

Irritated with herself and the world in general, she decided to walk into Kingston to get some hardware Trudy needed for minor repairs. She pulled a light blue windbreaker over her jeans and shirt, then headed out the door.

It was a little over a mile to the center of town, and she enjoyed the walk. The September weather had been unusually mild this year. The skies were clear and blue with only an occasional puffy cloud. The temperature hovered in the sixties, so she considered it near perfect.

Kingston was a small community, and its 5,000 residents were scattered far and wide. Federal grant funds were being used to renovate the town's historic buildings, so many of them were getting a much-needed face lift.

The downtown business area consisted of the city building, a professional office complex in converted, century-old structures, a fast food restaurant and a few small specialty shops.

Unfortunately, there was only one hardware store. As far as Katlyn was concerned, she'd prefer to never set foot inside Pete Pearson's Hardware again. Pete's wife, Dora, was the worst gossip within a hundred miles.

Devious Dora, as she had been nicknamed, had viciously maligned Jared the last time Katlyn had been in the store. It infuriated her every time she thought about it.

There were other places to get what she wanted, but Trudy preferred to use their account at Pearson's for business purchases. They liked supporting the local merchants, and Katlyn refused to be cowed by the old witch's meddling.

Lifting her chin and stiffening her spine, she entered the hardware store. As usual, the place was a beehive of activity, and Dora was manning the cash register near the door.

Katlyn ignored her, but greeted a few other acquaintances as she made her way through the aisles. It didn't take long to find the items she needed, so she collected them and carried them to the counter. Dora's greeting was frosty, her prune face puckered with displeasure as she handled the purchase.

Knowing everyone in the store was straining to see and hear their exchange made Katlyn uncomfortable, but there was nothing she could do to change human nature. There was no curiosity more avid than that in a close-knit community.

Dora slapped down a receipt for a signature, then her gaze shifted to someone else who'd approached the counter. Her expression grew even more disapproving.

A light touch at her waist and the tingling of sensual reaction alerted Katlyn to Jared's presence. She glanced up as he stepped close to her side. Suddenly Dora's self-righteous scowl didn't seem to matter anymore.

Her eyes lit with genuine warmth. "Hi there."

"Hi, yourself," he said, his gaze trapping hers. "You done here?"

"Yes, how about you?"

"I placed an order with Pete, so I'm done. How about joining me for a cup of coffee?"

Katlyn's smiled widened. "I'd like that."

She didn't give Dora a second thought, but she noticed that Jared flashed the older woman a dark glance. He wrapped a protective arm around Katlyn's waist and guided her outdoors.

As they started down the sidewalk, she asked, "What was that all about?"

"I didn't like that old battle-ax's attitude. She was rude to you."

"She's habitually rude. If she weren't Pete's wife, he probably would have fired her thirty years ago."

"Well, she'd better watch herself in the future," he declared grimly. "I told Pete if I ever hear of her discussing our private life or treating you with any disrespect, I'd cancel the ranch account permanently."

Katlyn stopped abruptly and stared at him in amazement. "You did what?"

Jared returned her stare with unflinching intensity. "You heard me. I told you I wouldn't tolerate anyone harassing you about our relationship, and I meant it."

"How did you know?" The words were out of her mouth before Katlyn realized how telling they were. She'd hoped he wouldn't learn about the unpleasant incident. She should have known better.

"Eli overheard the whole thing."

"Well, it sounds as though Eli is as big a gossip as Dora Pearson."

"Maybe," said Jared. "I gave him a warning, too. Where's your car?"

"I walked, and I'm not ready to end this discussion."

He turned her toward the store's parking lot. "My truck's over here. Do you need to go anywhere else?"

"Not really. I want to know exactly what Eli told you and what you said to Pete Pearson."

"Eli said old Dora was bad-mouthing me, and you told her to go suck an egg."

"I did not!"

Jared chuckled, amazing Katlyn. He sure seemed to be in a good mood; almost lighthearted. The idea was intriguing. She had a feeling it was a waste of time to argue with him, but she continued.

"I don't need you fighting my battles, and threatening the Pearsons was totally unnecessary. You don't have to throw your financial weight around on my account. It just adds fuel to the gossip."

Jared unlocked the passenger door of the truck, opening it for her.

"And what if I say I don't want you fighting my battles? Isn't that what you were doing when Devious Dora was maligning me?"

Katlyn opened her mouth to deny it, then snapped it shut again. Chalk one up for Jared. He was right, but that didn't make her feel any less argumentative. She changed the subject.

"Where are we going? I thought you wanted coffee."

Jared flashed her a rare, boyish grin and brushed a thumb over her cheek. "Not particularly. I just wanted you all to myself."

The grin, his touch and his outrageous words sent a ripple of excitement through Katlyn. All thoughts of arguing ceased.

She shook her head at his audacity, then climbed into the truck. He strode around to the driver's side, and her pulse accelerated when he slid into the cab. He was so big and masculine and exciting to be near.

The heavy air in the truck seemed to pulse with the power of his presence. She allowed herself an instant of sensual delight. Then she remembered he hadn't contacted her for two days.

"What brings you to town in the middle of a weekday morning?"

Jared threw a glance at her as he pulled out of the parking lot, and she realized that the sudden coolness in her tone betrayed her real emotions— which were anything but cool.

"I just got back from Casper," he explained. "Did you miss me?"

She shrugged, unwilling to let him know just how much she'd missed him.

"I had a call from my lawyer Sunday afternoon and spent all day yesterday in court. My ex-stepmother has finally run out of appeals. The case was thrown out for insufficient grounds."

Katlyn abruptly forgot her grievances. "Jared! That's great. I'm so happy for you," she enthused, turning to face him more fully. "Does this mean you're finally, completely free of your father's ex-wife?"

He shot her another broad grin. "The judge said if she tried any more legal tricks she'd get thrown in jail for contempt. He accused her of wasting taxpayers' time and money. He's tired of her attempts to manipulate the system, and he's making her pay all the legal and court fees."

"Wow! Jared, that's the very best you could have hoped for."

After spending the past three years embroiled in expensive legal battles, it had to be a tremendous relief for him. Now she understood his almost jubilant mood.

"Maybe you're truly rid of her this time!"

"I hope so."

They'd reached Katlyn's house, and he parked the truck under a big shade tree behind the garage. They were fairly hidden from view, so she eased closer and touched his arm.

"Would you like to come inside? I can make coffee or whatever you'd like."

Jared shoved her back to her side of the seat and followed, pressing close and sliding his arms around her.

"Like I said before," he whispered hoarsely, "all I want is you."

His mouth came down to cover hers with a consuming hunger that stole her breath. She moaned softly, then savored the kiss to the fullest. When he thrust his tongue deep into her mouth, she sucked it greedily, inflamed by the force of his need.

A low groan rumbled from his chest. His hands slid to her hips. He flexed long fingers into her denim covered flesh, then lifted and shifted her until she was straddling his thighs.

The rest of the world faded away as she savored the spicy sweetness of his desire. His tongue swept the softness of her mouth and then coaxed her to reciprocate. When she offered her tongue, he sucked it until she felt the pull of desire deep in the pit of her stomach.

Katlyn shifted restlessly in his lap. She couldn't get close enough to soothe the growing ache between her thighs. She murmured an almost inaudible protest into his mouth.

Their lips parted, and they gasped for air.

"I know," he grumbled. "I want more, too. I want you hard and fast, then long and slow and easy. I want you where I can feel every inch of you against every inch of me."

Katlyn shuddered at the hot promise in his tone. Her bones turned to mush, and her body flowed more fully against his. She felt the rigid strength of his need and tried to assuage her own by rubbing against it.

Jared groaned again as his hips bucked and his lips made a foray beneath her hair to scatter kisses along her neck and throat.

Katlyn shuddered at the exquisite pleasure, and shivers ran down her spine.

"Any chance your house is deserted?" he murmured into her ear.

"Trudy was at the restaurant when I left." Her reply was punctuated with breathy sighs. "But she comes and goes all the time."

He mumbled an inarticulate complaint. "Then come home with me and help me celebrate a little."

The husky invitation made her quiver with longing. She was tempted, so tempted, but common sense prevailed.

"I have to go to work in a little while."

"Play hooky," he urged while nibbling on the sensitive skin of her neck.

"I can't," she insisted weakly, "there's nobody to replace me."

Jared's breathing was rough. He pressed his forehead against hers, and she knew he was fighting for control. His hands clutched the top of her thighs while he nudged her closer to his straining erection.

"Damn, Katlyn, I can't take much more of this. Do you get your kicks with this teasing?"

Katlyn's breath hitched, and pain gripped her chest. "Is that what you think? I'm a tease?"

"Maybe not deliberately, but you sure as hell leave me aching."

Stung, she squirmed to free herself from his grip, her tone growing heated. "If all you want is someone to scratch an itch, then I guess you need to look somewhere else!"

"Hey, this is your fault," he tossed back at her. Raking a hand through his hair, he continued, "You're the one who's playing games. But I know exactly what I want."

"Sex!" She shifted awkwardly to her own side of the cab.

"Damned straight," he snapped, sliding beneath the wheel. "A lot of it, and I'm honest enough to admit it."

"Meaning what?" she asked while straightening her clothes. "That I'm dishonest because I don't want to jump into bed with you?"

"Dishonest because you *do* want to jump in bed with me; you just don't want to admit it."

His accusation touched a raw nerve. He was right,

but admitting it, even to herself, only heightened her anger and frustration.

They glared at each other for a few long, heated moments. Then Katlyn opened the door, jumped from the truck, and slammed it closed in a fit of temper. The same temper fired her up as she marched to the house.

Jared revved the truck's engine to life, reversed from the drive and pulled onto the street with a squeal of tires, but she didn't watch him leave.

She went inside the house and headed straight for the kitchen. At the sink, she drew herself a glass of water. Her throat was dry, her hands shaking, and her stomach rolling. Worse, she felt the stinging threat of tears.

Blinking furiously, she chastised herself for being such a wimp. She'd never been the type to cry over every little upset, and she hated it, hated the emotional upheaval.

Forcing herself to breathe deeply, she gazed out the window toward the road, and tried to regain some control. Then she began to chastise herself because she missed Jared before he was a mile down the road.

Who was she trying to fool? What was she trying to prove by resisting her need for him? If she didn't stop pushing him away, how long would it be before he got fed up and found someone more willing?

A tremulous sigh escaped her. She loved him. Hopelessly. Unconditionally. She'd given him her heart and soul along with her body.

When she'd left him, she'd believed it was the right thing to do; the safe, sane thing to do. The memories would always be precious, but she'd thought she could go back to her independent life-style and get over him. She'd been oh-so-wrong.

All she'd learned was that she couldn't bear the thought of life without him. So why was she subjecting them both to this emotional roller coaster?

Maybe he didn't feel the same undying devotion. Maybe he never would. That wasn't likely to change how she felt about him, so why wasn't she cultivating his love rather than constantly pushing him away?

Unable to supply a logical answer to her own question, she reached a decision. With it came the feeling of a heavy weight lifting from her shoulders. Breathing easier, she wiped a stray teardrop from her cheek.

They could work out a compromise that would allow them to be together, but also allow her to maintain some independence and self-respect.

The thought of following Jared home to share the decision with him was tempting, but she restrained the urge. There was no sense in setting a bad precedent. It would have to wait until after work. Then she could go to him with a clear conscience.

Throughout her shift that evening, Katlyn prayed Jared hadn't turned to another woman to satisfy his needs. Her eyes regularly drifted to the dining room, but he didn't make an appearance, even a late one. By closing time, her nerves were frayed.

Feeling tired and grimy, she reconsidered her earlier plan to show up at his house unannounced. Instead, she went home and took a shower. Then she slipped into a comfortable cotton nightgown and curled up in bed.

It took a few more minutes to bolster her courage. Finally, at half past ten, she reached for the phone and punched in Jared's number. Trudy always insisted that calling anyone after nine was ill-mannered, but Katlyn chose to ignore that particular social rule at the moment.

Her heart pounded as she listened to the first ring, hardly believing her jitters. This was worse than anything she'd experienced as a teenager. Of course, this was the first time she'd ever called anyone to revive a love affair.

Another ring. What if he was already asleep? What if he refused to talk to her? Her palms were sweating. What if he had someone with him?

After the third ring, Katlyn started to hang up the receiver. Then the ringing abruptly stopped.

"King."

The sound of his voice made her stomach muscles clench. Her words came out weak and hesitant. "Jared, it's Katlyn. I hope I didn't wake you."

A pause, and then, "You didn't wake me."

She twisted the phone cord through her fingers as an awkward silence fell. His tone neither encouraged nor discouraged. The indifference was even worse.

"Did you have a late night?"

He could interpret her interest in several ways, but Katlyn figured the only way to learn what she wanted to know was to ask.

"Dan asked for the afternoon off, so I was late getting chores done."

That could explain why he hadn't come to the restaurant. "Did you get something to eat?"

"A sandwich."

His response was muffled, and Katlyn panicked. Was someone with him? What was he doing?

"Is this a bad time?"

Jared's voice came through strong again. "Just towel-drying my hair. I was in the shower when the phone rang."

"Sorry," Katlyn's voice quivered slightly as she envisioned him straight from the shower. He always wrapped one towel around his hips and used another to blot the moisture from his hair. Then he tossed them both aside. "I wasn't sure if it was too late to call."

"No problem. I just wanted to get dry enough to get in bed."

She closed her eyes, and swallowed a small moan. It was too easy to envision his gloriously naked body sliding between the sheets. The dark hair on his broad chest would be glistening, swirling silkily around taut male nipples.

His washboard stomach would ripple as he stretched out hard thighs and long legs. Then there were the exclusively male parts. The memories brought heat to her flesh.

"Are you still there?" he asked.

"Sorry again," Katlyn replied with candor, even though her tone had gone husky. "I got distracted by thoughts of you stretching out in bed."

There was another brief pause, then his tone held a wealth of masculine challenge. "Well, I'm buck naked."

She sighed, curled into a ball and buried one side of her face in the pillow. "I guessed as much."

"Are you in bed?"

"Yes."

His tone roughened. "Naked?"

"No. I'm wearing my old lavender nightgown."

"The short, transparent one?"

Katlyn laughed softly. "It's not supposed to be transparent."

"It is, but I wasn't complaining. I'd like to see it right now."

Her breathing faltered. "Would you?"

"See it, feel it, touch you through it," he insisted gruffly.

"Touch me?" Katlyn's voice was barely audible as her senses went haywire. "How would you touch me?"

The line went quiet as he hesitated. She knew he wasn't used to talking about his needs, but she held her breath in hopes he'd try.

Six

"What would you most like to touch?" Katlyn coaxed. "Humor me, and tell me what you'd do if we were together right now."

Jared finally answered, his voice raspy as he put his needs into words. "I'd hold your breasts first and fill my hands with their softness."

His response titillated her; both physically and emotionally. Her breasts swelled. She wanted him to talk to her, to learn to share his feelings, but she didn't know if she could stand it.

"I'd like that. What next?"

"Then I'd brush my thumbs back and forth over your nipples until they were hard as rocks, and you started making those sweet little noises."

Katlyn's nipples tightened just as he suggested. The rest of her was going liquid. She smothered the sounds of arousal with her pillow. Teaching Jared to communicate could prove more painful than she'd expected.

Once started, he showed no mercy. "I might lick them through the fabric, but I'd have to get your gown out of the way quick. I'd want to suck you deep into my mouth and taste you with my tongue."

She swallowed a tiny whimper.

"And while I'm doing that, I'd want to touch your

bare thighs and feel the muscles quiver in my hands."

"Jared!" Katlyn curled into a tight ball and abruptly forgot about lessons in communication.

"That's what I'd want to hear," he added with masculine satisfaction. "You begging for more. Your fingers would be locked in my hair, and you'd be twisting and turning on the bed. I'd have to throw a leg over your hips to hold you still."

Katlyn could almost feel the weight of his leg and the subtle rasp of wiry hair against her flesh. The muscles in her legs twitched restlessly. She couldn't stand much more. He was quickly getting the upper hand in this conversation. It was time to go on the offensive.

"Then I'd have to let go of your hair and slide my hands down your shoulders and arms," she said. "I'd sink my fingers into your hips and tug you closer."

It was Jared's turn to utter a low growl of arousal. Katlyn quivered in response to the desire in his voice.

"I'd want to kiss your chest and stomach and every tiny inch of you."

"Tiny?" he swiftly objected.

She laughed and clarified. "Every inch of you, big or small, hard or soft."

"Most of me's pretty hard right now."

Katlyn could visualize every deliciously responsive inch of him. "Really?"

"Real hard."

She chuckled, and he responded with another low growl.

"Did you call just to get me all hot and bothered, or was there something else on you mind?"

"Just you."

They were quiet for a few seconds as they shared the simple knowledge.

"Miss me tonight?"

Katlyn knew it was a hard question for him to ask. It was an admission of caring, but she didn't want to make a big deal of it.

"Kinda," she replied.

He took offense. "Kinda?"

"A little."

"Just a little?"

"Maybe a lot."

"You ran me off this morning."

That could be another admission of caring, but she had no way of telling if it was genuine hurt or just a bruised ego.

"I know. I'm sorry. I almost followed you, but I had to work."

"If you'd followed me, we'd be lovers again." His tone left no doubt.

"I know."

"I thought you couldn't accept that."

"So did I."

"But?" he demanded swiftly.

"But I've changed my mind." There—she'd admitted it. The real purpose for her call. She heard Jared suck in a breath before replying.

"You're sure?"

"I'm sure I miss you and want to be with you when I can."

"You'll move back in with me?" His question was swift, his tone demanding.

"No," came her equally swift denial. "We can have an affair if you want, but I won't live with you. I want to work. I know my schedule's weird, but we can find a way."

He'd have to accept the compromise or forget the affair. Katlyn held her breath, knowing he wouldn't be totally satisfied with her plan.

"Do you ever have days off?"

The breath slowly eased from her lungs in relief, and a smile echoed in her response. "It just happens that tomorrow is my day off this week."

"I've already taken too much time off this week. I have a lot of work that needs doing."

"Let me help." She held her breath again, awaiting his response. In the past, he hadn't wanted her involved in the running of the ranch, had refused to consider it.

"I don't have any experience, but surely an extra pair of hands can be of some help." She hated to plead, but his decision was too important to let pride get in the way.

After what seemed a painfully long pause, he asked her another question.

"Can you ride?"

His capitulation delighted her. It was a small victory, but an important one.

"I was practically born in the saddle," she fudged. Ryan Havens had taught her years ago, but it didn't seem judicious to mention his name. Surely she could remember the basics.

"Can you be out here by six?"

Katlyn moaned. "As in six A.M.?"

A chuckle teased her through the lines. "You said you wanted to help. That's when I start work."

She turned over in bed and reached for her alarm clock, setting it for five-thirty. That done, she switched off her light, slid back in bed and hugged the phone to her ear.

"You still there?" asked Jared.

"I was setting my alarm."

"You'd better get some sleep."

"I know." She was physically exhausted, but didn't want to sever the connection with him. "You need some rest, too."

"Planning on wearing me out tomorrow?" he asked, his tone going low and suggestive again.

It sent a quiver of longing through Katlyn and made her wish she'd gone to him tonight. She burrowed deeper into the bed and whispered back to him. "You might need all your strength and stamina." Which was considerable. Just remembering made her blood run hot.

"Is that a promise?"

"Uh-huh."

"Tomorrow," he said softly.

"Tomorrow."

At six the next morning, Jared finished his coffee and rinsed the cup out in the sink. He glanced at the clock and then silently cursed. He'd been watching the damn thing for an hour. Waiting for Katlyn.

He hadn't expected to sleep, yet he'd gone out like a light as soon as he'd hung up the phone. It was the first good night's sleep he'd had in weeks. He'd awakened with replays of their conversation monopolizing his thoughts.

She'd agreed to be lovers again. He felt a surge

of elation every time he thought about it. Hunger too long denied was eating at him like a disease.

He resented the need and had fought it. Had even considered seeking satisfaction elsewhere. There were women who'd welcome the chance to take Katlyn's place in his bed, but he wanted her.

She was late. He'd said six, and she hadn't showed yet. With each minute, his tension increased. Had she changed her mind again? Balked at telling her aunt where she was going? Had Trudy convinced her it was wrong to come?

He cursed and glanced at the clock again. It was ten past. Dan would be here soon, ready to start work, and he'd wanted some time alone with Katlyn.

A sweep of headlights through the window made him stiffen. He listened to make sure the vehicle wasn't his foreman's truck. When the engine shut off, he moved toward the door to watch her approach.

His blood ran hot at the sight of her. The way she filled out a pair of jeans could incite a riot, and her slow, rolling walk could drive a man crazy just watching. Especially one who had intimate knowledge of her sensuous moves.

She was his. He'd never been a possessive man where women were concerned, but he couldn't deny that his feelings were more complex when it came to Katlyn. He had no desire to analyze them. He just wanted her.

"Sorry I'm late," she offered when he opened the door. "I kept dozing after the alarm woke me."

Jared slowly pulled her into the house and straight into his arms. She still looked warm and flushed from sleep. Blood rushed to his groin.

"It'll cost you a kiss," he insisted, tugging her close.

She met him halfway. Her lips were soft, yet seductively responsive. She tasted sweetly tart, like mint.

He pressed her mouth open wider with his. Their kisses grew longer and deeper, until they were both gasping for air.

"If that's a penance, I think I'll have to be late more often," Katlyn murmured against his mouth.

Jared sank his fingers into the silky softness of her hair and studied her upturned face. "You look sleepy."

"Uh-huh."

"And sexy as hell."

Her smile was sultry. "You think?"

"I know." He slid his hands to her hips and pulled her closer, rubbing his hardness against her softness. "Too well, I know."

"Complaining?"

"Not as long as you haven't changed your mind." A thread of steel entered his tone. "No more games."

She stiffened instantly and tried to pull free from his hold. He didn't let her.

"I was never playing games, Jared," she insisted, staring at him with unblinking honesty.

Maybe she believed that, but he didn't, and he didn't want to argue about it. They weren't likely to agree in a hundred years.

The sound of another vehicle entering the drive caught their attention. "That'll be Dan. It's time to head out to the barn. Are you sure you want to work or would you rather just make yourself at home until I get done?"

Katlyn frowned, and he continued. "I can try to be back by noon, if you'd like to sleep a while longer."

"Why are you so reluctant to let me help?" she demanded.

He didn't want to discuss his objections. "I don't help you cook at the restaurant, do I?"

"No, but then you've never offered. I certainly wouldn't mind. I'm not so territorial that I don't welcome help."

"Territorial?" Did she mean about the ranch or about her?

"You always act like I'm invading your privacy if I mention looking around the ranch. Are you afraid I'm going to calculate the value of everything? Or are you embarrassed to introduce me to your crew?"

He ignored the taunt about calculating the ranch's worth. In his experience, women always did just that.

"Embarrassed? More like worried. Beautiful women have a way of messing with men's concentration."

He started to open the door again, but Katlyn clutched his arm, demanding attention. Her eyes were wide with entreaty as she gazed up at him.

"You think I'm beautiful?"

The vulnerability of her expression stopped him in his tracks. She wasn't fishing for compliments, she was begging for reassurance. Her eyes were so big and guileless that he felt an unwelcome tightness in his chest.

"You know you're beautiful."

"You've never said so."

"Oh, hell." Jared frowned, trying to remember. He'd shown her in a hundred ways that he found her attractive. Did it matter if he'd never said the words?

"Never." Her insistence was firm.

"Do you need compliments?" he grumbled, annoyed with himself for not recognizing her insecurities. Most of the women he knew were all too aware of their feminine charms.

"It might be nice to have some verbal communication occasionally," she insisted, shifting to put some distance between them. "Something besides 'I want you in my bed.'"

Jared shoved his hair back and slid his hat on his head. There was no use arguing about his communication skills again. He had work to do, and arguing was a waste of valuable time.

"Are you coming with me or staying inside?"

"With you," she snapped. "And I'll try to look as ugly as I can so as not to disturb anyone's concentration."

She would disturb him. There was no doubt in his mind. She always did when she was near, but he wasn't about to let her spend the day with anyone else.

He'd just have to divide his attention, keep a close eye on her and see that his men kept their distance. He'd never met a woman who could resist flirting when she was alone with a group of men.

They met Dan in the driveway and exchanged greetings. Then the other man offered to start her car for her.

"I'm coming, not going."

Jared watched the blush warm her cheeks. She'd quickly corrected Dan's misconception, but her embarrassment irritated him. She had no reason to feel guilty about spending time with him.

"Katlyn's going to help today."

Dan's expression registered surprise and then easy acceptance. "Sounds good. We can use all the help we can get."

She smiled. "I don't know much about ranching, but I'm willing to learn."

Jared remembered her words several times over the next few hours. As they saddled up and rode around the ranch, Katlyn showed a genuine interest in its workings. She bombarded him with questions, and he enjoyed sharing his love of the land with her.

The morning passed swiftly as they searched for stray cattle. The herds were being moved closer to the barns for winter, so they were checking all over the ranch for stragglers.

The sun was directly overhead before it occurred to him that five hours in the saddle were too much for a novice. They were herding a small batch of cows toward the barns, so he eased his horse close enough to talk again.

"How you doin'?"

Katlyn gave him a smile. "I'm fine, but I'm probably going to be sore tomorrow."

"I forgot about that," he admitted, then grinned. "I'll have to rub some liniment on the tender spots."

She rolled her eyes, and his breath caught at their beauty. They sparkled with amusement and happi-

ness. Even though she'd been coughing from the
dust they'd stirred up all morning, she hadn't complained once. She seemed to be enjoying herself.

Desire, sharp and unexpected, clawed at him. He
wanted to touch her, to pull her off the horse and
lose himself in her. The need was so fierce, so driving, that it shook him to the core.

He needed time to get control. "I can finish here.
Why don't you head for the house?"

"You sure you don't mind?"

"I'm sure."

"Would you like me to fix some lunch?"

"It's your day off. Just rest. I'll be in shortly."

"What about Sasha?" she asked, patting her
mount's neck.

"Turn her loose in the corral. I'll take care of
her."

"You really don't mind?"

He nodded, and she finally reined the mare toward the house, then nudged Sasha into a canter.
She had a gentle touch, looked good in the saddle
and had been a really good sport all morning.

Maybe he should have invited her to help when
she'd lived with him. He'd been wrong in thinking
she wouldn't fit in. Problem was, he hadn't wanted
to share her attention with anyone or anything,
which made his need for her seem almost obsessive.

The only other thing he'd ever felt so strongly
about was this ranch. People had come and gone,
but the love of this land was in his heart and soul.
He was the sixth generation of Kings to own the
property, so a little obsession didn't seem abnormal.
What he felt for Katlyn defied the norm.

He was close enough to see Eli greet her as she

rode into the ranch yard. After stopping near the corral, the younger man offered her a hand. She accepted help dismounting, paused a minute, then headed straight for the house.

Katlyn had been polite and friendly when introduced to his staff. Eli was the only one who'd dared to flirt, but she'd smoothly discouraged him without causing hard feelings. Jared supposed she'd had a lot of practice dodging unwanted attention.

The thought brought another rush of possessiveness. He was glad she didn't wait tables anymore, so she didn't have to fend off advances. Some men around these parts still thought that patronizing a restaurant entitled them to special favors from the staff.

Irritated by his train of thought, he turned his attention back to the cattle. Dan and another ranch hand were herding a small group of strays toward him so that they could all be driven toward pastures closer to the barn.

Jared kept a tight rein on his patience and forced himself to concentrate on the job at hand. The roundup continued smoothly, but it was still another hour before he could free himself long enough to join her.

The house was quiet as he entered from the back porch and moved through the kitchen. He opened the refrigerator for something cold to drink and found a tray of sandwiches. A call to Katlyn went unanswered, so he guessed she was upstairs. Smiling, he carried the plate and two cans of cola to his bedroom.

He found her fast asleep on his bed with her back to the door. She'd showered and put on one of his white T-shirts. Nothing else. It clung lovingly to the curves of her waist, hips and thighs.

A rush of heat hit him hard, knocking the air from his lungs. His hands shook as he set the food on the bedside table, his fingers clenching at the sight of her dark hair tumbling across his pillow. A slow perusal of her long, bare legs made his pulse leap wildly.

Kicking off his boots, he jerked off the rest of his clothes and headed for the shower. His patience was already sorely tested, so he didn't waste time. Within five minutes, he was drying his body and tossing aside the towels.

Katlyn lay on her right side, so he eased himself into bed facing her. Then he gathered her in his arms and drew her closer. She mumbled sleepily and snuggled against him, causing his heart to thud heavily against his ribs.

For a long time, he simply enjoyed the feel of her soft, warm body. He inhaled the clean, sweet smell of her, filling his senses with her unique scent. Then he traced the delicate features of her face with his thumb before running his fingers through her hair.

So soft, so sweet, so sexy. Beautiful.

Everything about her was beautiful. Surely she didn't have any doubts about her looks. How could he have thought it so often, yet never said it out loud? Why would that make her feel insecure and defensive?

He didn't have the answers; didn't want to think about it now. More pressing needs prompted bolder caresses. He slid his hands to her bare thighs and began to gently massage the muscles that would be sore from riding. The flesh was firm yet satisfyingly soft.

His fingers kneaded the supple flesh as he nudged her closer. Finally, her lashes fluttered, eyes opening as she gazed directly into his.

"Hi," she whispered softly, giving him an intimate smile that made his chest muscles constrict.

His voice was a husky whisper, too. "Hi yourself."

"I fell asleep."

"I noticed."

Her gaze never left his, but her hands began to wander over his chest, her fingers threading through the tight curls.

"I borrowed a T-shirt."

"I noticed that, too."

"Without asking permission," she confessed.

"You're a wicked woman."

Katlyn nodded solemnly, eyes wide. "I guess you'll want it back."

"Uh-huh," he muttered as he continued to caress her thighs. "You'll have to give it back."

"Right now?"

"Yeah." His reply was little more than a rasp as her fingers found his nipples.

He slid his hands up her body, taking the shirt with them. Then he pulled it off her arms, over her head and tossed it to the floor.

"Another penance?" she asked hopefully.

"The one for borrowing T-shirts without asking is even tougher than the one for being late."

"Oh my."

She nibbled on his chin, her teeth and lips creating havoc with his self-control.

"I might have to punish you for hours," he threatened.

"Oh!" Her teasing exclamation turned into a sigh of pleasure as he hugged her closer.

Her skin was as smooth as a newborn babe's. He liked the feel of it against his palms as he slowly caressed the curve of her spine. He sunk his fingers into the taut flesh of her buttocks and tugged her tight against his erection.

Then they swallowed each other's moans as he locked his mouth with hers. He plunged his tongue deep into the luscious depths; tasting, stroking, desperate to assuage his hunger for her.

Katlyn's arms slid over his shoulders and grasped the back of his head to hold him tight. She returned his kisses with an eagerness that set him on fire.

Her breasts pressed against his chest, her nipples brushing pleasurably against his as she eased one of her legs between his thighs. He dragged his mouth from hers and made a trail of swift, hard kisses down her neck to her breasts.

He eased his grip on her just enough to suck a nipple into his mouth, nipping and tonguing it until it pebbled tightly. When he gave the other breast equal attention, she started making those mewing sounds of arousal he loved. It made him ravenous for her mouth again.

This time their kisses were more rough and wet. Their tongues dueled and demanded.

Jared had promised himself to go slowly, to give her a loving she'd never forget, but his control was shattering with every sound and move she made. It had been too long. Blood pounded impatiently in his head and his groin. He was on the verge of erupting.

Dragging his mouth from Katlyn's, he barely managed to speak. "Are you protected?"

"No."

Her response had him groaning. She'd gone on birth control pills when they'd been together, but must have quit taking them. He was glad she'd been celibate, but he hated having to use protection now.

Reaching toward a shelf in the headboard, he grabbed a condom and ripped the foil with his teeth as she tugged gently at one of his nipples. His hips jerked involuntarily as her fingers slid down to help him.

"Damn, don't touch me or I'll explode," he warned.

Her sexy, unrepentant chuckle sent a shudder over him. He was trembling and losing control. He knew Katlyn wasn't ready yet, so he slid a hand between her legs and caressed her as he pressed her flat on her back.

He teased her nipples once more with his tongue, then gradually shifted his weight onto his forearms as he positioned himself over her.

Their gazes met and locked as he nudged her thighs apart and settled himself between them. Then he watched her eyes dilate as he thrust into her, burying himself deeply in her tight, moist heat.

Another shudder racked his body as he dragged air into his lungs. He struggled for control when she wrapped her legs around his hips, but lost it as soon as she began to move. All thoughts of slow and easy evaporated in a rush of white-hot desire.

Seven

"Sorry I was so impatient."

Katlyn smiled. Tucked in the curve of Jared's arm, snug against his warm body, she was feeling sated and secure. It was easy to forgive his impatience. She liked the idea of challenging his formidable self-control.

"I was a little impatient, too."

"Were you?" he asked as he turned on his side and faced her again.

The afternoon sun shone through the window, lighting on naked, glistening bodies still warm from exertion. Jared's dark eyes were half-closed, giving him a look of intense concentration rather than the sated exhaustion she was feeling.

He slid his hands to her hips and tugged her closer. She reached out and traced the strong line of his chin with one finger.

"You make me impatient," she accused.

"Is that a complaint?"

Katlyn stretched until she could capture his mouth with her own. Thinking that showing was better than telling, she offered him a kiss that was long and slow and satisfying. When they finally needed air, she drew back slightly, but not before bathing his lips with her tongue.

A low growl rumbled from his throat, and his fingers flexed convulsively on her hips.

She regretted never taking the initiative during their loving. At first, she'd been too inexperienced. She'd been content to wallow in Jared's attentions. Now she had weeks' worth of cravings to satisfy.

"Do you have to go back to work this afternoon?" she asked, beginning to explore his big body with her hands.

"Yeah."

"Too bad," she cooed. "I wanted to ravish you for the rest of the day."

"Ravish?" The word was pressed against her neck along with his kisses. "What did you have in mind?"

The keen interest in his tone emboldened Katlyn. She shoved him backward until he was flat on the bed. Then she began leaving slow, meandering kisses all over his warm flesh.

Jared sank his fingers in her hair, but didn't try to slow her or guide her. His nipples tightened into hard little nubs as she licked them, taking great pleasure in the taste and texture.

His chest heaved and his stomach muscles rippled as her kisses progressed downward. She wasn't feeling quite bold enough to caress the part of him already growing erect, but her mouth skirted close, then moved on to his thighs.

After kissing her way down his legs, she took his feet in her hands, massaging the arches as she silently urged him to turn over so that she could explore his backside with equal attention.

By the time she'd worked her way over his firm buttocks to his broad shoulders, she was lying on top of him, flesh to flesh again. Her nipples ached, so she rubbed them against his back. She rocked her pelvis against his taut buttocks, then sank her teeth into the curve of his shoulders and sucked greedily.

The tremor that racked Jared's body gave her a wild thrill of excitement. She basked in the feminine power, but quickly found herself flat on her back with him looming over her.

"My turn," he demanded, his voice rough with arousal.

He took her mouth with barely leashed hunger, drinking his fill. His hands were molding the fullness of her breasts, his thumbs teasing the nipples until he could replace them with his lips. Then he sucked one while gently plucking at the other.

Fire raced through Katlyn; blistering hot and engulfing, making her shift restlessly on the bed. She clutched at Jared's shoulders, trying to tug him over her, but he refused the satisfaction she craved.

"Not yet, sweetheart. I want equal time."

She moaned as his hand slid to the cradle of her thighs, offering only partial satisfaction as he stroked her intimately. She arched closer to his touch and writhed against his hard fingers.

Clutching fistfuls of his hair, she coaxed him on. "Please, Jared!"

He would not be hurried, but continued to plant hot, wet kisses down her stomach. When his mouth replaced his teasing fingers, Katlyn nearly came off the bed. Her body bowed, and she cried out as his lips and tongue drove her higher and higher.

"I want you!"

In response, Jared wrapped his arms around her hips and pulled her closer to his mouth. Every nerve in her body sizzled with erotic heat. A scream of pure pleasure escaped as she spiraled toward a shattering release.

She cried out as she went limp on the bed, breathing raggedly and certain she'd never be able to move again. Feeling drained, she wanted to pull Jared over her, but didn't have the strength.

He didn't seem inclined to satisfy his own need, but continued to caress her. He kissed his way down her thighs and calves, his hands and mouth both massaging.

Exhausted, Katlyn remained limp as Jared turned her on her stomach and began to stroke and kiss her backside just as she'd done to him. She didn't think it was humanly possible to become aroused again, but she was wrong. As his strong fingers stroked her flesh, she felt heat building within her again.

A shiver danced down her spine when his mouth locked onto the back of her neck. She felt her nipples tighten and her stomach clench. Then Jared pulled her against him, spoon fashion, and reached between her legs again. She gasped as he swiftly brought her to another, more stunning release.

Trembling, Katlyn turned in his arms, and tried to pull him over her again. She wanted to give him the same blissful satisfaction he'd given her.

Still he resisted, so she stopped trying and let him have his way with her. She lost track of time as he relentlessly drove her from one peak to another. Giving herself totally to his mercy, she stopped thinking and just surrendered to the sensual pleasure only he could give.

Eventually, he lost control of his own desire and

joined his body with hers to make them whole
again. Katlyn clung to him until they reached the
heights together. Then, replete and exhausted, she
slept.

Hours later, she awoke to a bedroom darkened
by late afternoon shadows. Jared was gone, but he'd
pulled the covers over her naked body. She
stretched, feeling totally decadent as the sheets
brushed against her sensitized flesh.

She'd lived with him for several weeks, yet he'd
never made love to her the way he had today.
They'd been insatiable in the past, but passion and
impatience had often overridden the sensuality.

Today, he'd given her a uniquely erotic experience that she'd never forget. Parts of her body were
already tingling and craving more.

Had that been Jared's intention? To try and bind
her to him with his incredibly skillful lovemaking?
Did he think she'd had complaints with the physical
aspects of their relationship? Like most other men,
did everything boil down to sex as far as he was
concerned?

Katlyn sat up in bed and her stomach rolled. She
glanced toward the bedside stand where Jared had
left a sandwich and a cola. The thought of either
made her queasy, yet she knew she needed something to eat.

She hadn't eaten anything all day. The hours on
horseback in the sun had made her slightly ill and
lightheaded, but she'd have died before admitting
it. All she'd wanted earlier was a shower and to lie

down. Now she wanted a shower and something to settle the rumbling in her stomach.

Climbing from bed, she tidied the covers and picked up the discarded T-shirt she'd been wearing. A glance in the bathroom mirror confirmed that she was sunburnt and more than a little tousled.

After her shower, she slipped into Jared's shirt again, loving the feel and scent of it against her skin. Then she headed for the utility room and transferred her clothes from the washer to the dryer.

Lastly, she entered the big yellow and white kitchen with all its modern appliances. Comfortably at home in the familiar surroundings, she quickly gathered the fixings for an easy dinner.

Within an hour, spaghetti sauce was simmering, water was boiling for the pasta and garlic bread was ready for the oven. She was setting the table and singing along with the radio when she sensed Jared's presence.

She turned to find him standing just inside the kitchen door. Arms crossed in his favorite stance, he was leaning against the doorjamb. His gaze was locked on her.

"Hi," seemed all she could say as a wave of intense emotion washed over her.

His worn, faded jeans and thin red T-shirt boldly displayed every fascinating line of his lean form. Looking at him was like touching a live wire. Every nerve in her body sizzled. Her blood heated along with her cheeks.

"Hi, yourself."

The deep intimacy of his tone threatened her equilibrium even more. Suddenly, Katlyn was giddy and tongue-tied. She dragged her gaze from him and tried to regain some calm, but was unable to think of a single thing to say.

"Smells good in here." Jared offered her a safe topic.

"I hope you don't mind my cooking. I guess it's just a habit with me, even on my day off. I was hungry and knew you would be too."

"What's to mind?" he said. "A beautiful woman singing in the kitchen while she cooks? It sure beats coming home to a quiet, empty house."

Katlyn trembled and her throat clogged with annoying tears. It was as close as Jared had come to saying he'd really missed her; missed more than just her body in his bed. She'd often wondered if he got lonely or just preferred his solitude.

"I still have to cook the spaghetti and bread. How soon would you like to eat?"

She dared a glance at him again and found his gaze riveted on her. It roamed slowly over her body, causing more heat. Then their gazes locked, and he spoke in a voice that left no doubt about the direction of his thoughts.

"I'd like to give you a proper hello right now, but I'm filthy. It won't take me more than a few minutes to jump in the shower."

She offered him a shaky smile. "I was so dusty that I threw my clothes in the washer, but they should be dry by now. I'm afraid I borrowed your shirt again without asking."

Jared slowly moved closer. "The penance this time is that you have to keep it on, but get rid of those underthings."

More heat washed over Katlyn. She'd put on her

clean underwear even though her jeans hadn't been dry enough yet. He'd obviously noticed. The thought of being naked under the shirt while they shared a meal seemed deliciously wanton.

"Deal?" He was urging her not to turn shy.

"Only if you do the same," she countered with a bravado she didn't quite feel. "I can stand it if you can."

Jared flashed her another simmering glance and then headed upstairs to his room. Katlyn watched him leave, and an erotic shiver ran through her. He certainly had a way of keeping her off balance.

When she finally managed to move, she put bread in the oven and spaghetti into the boiling water. Then she slipped into the utility room and slipped out of her underwear.

Her nipples jutted against the soft, blue fabric, making her feel exposed and vulnerable. Wearing nothing but a shirt felt all right in bed, but not so in the kitchen. She started to put her things back on, then hesitated and changed her mind again.

The indecision was indicative of her relationship with Jared. Her emotions were in constant turmoil. Loving him was like one very exhilarating, fabulous, frightening roller-coaster ride. The highs were incredibly high; the lows the absolute pits.

Mentally commanding herself to be more daring and spontaneous, she returned to the kitchen just in time to keep the spaghetti water from boiling all over the stove.

For the next ten minutes, she put the finishing touches on their dinner. After pouring them both some wine, she drained the pasta and checked the bread. Bending to remove it from the oven without baring her rear end was a challenge, but she managed.

She turned to put it on the table and found Jared's gaze fixed on her again. She hadn't heard him approach, but that wasn't surprising. He was barefoot. Except for a pair of snug jean cutoffs, the rest of him was gloriously naked, too.

Katlyn couldn't help staring. She loved the way his dark hair swirled down his chest and stomach. Her gaze flitted to the front of his cutoffs and took note of the bulge behind his zipper. The flush from the heat of the oven bloomed into a full-blown blush of desire.

"Wondering if I have anything on under my jeans?" he drawled in mocking challenge.

"Do you?" she managed in a choked whisper.

"That's for me to know and you to find out."

Katlyn put the bread on the table and started toward him, but he warded her off with both hands.

"Not now," he insisted, giving her a wickedly amused grin. "I'm starved, so I'm not letting this meal get ruined."

Since she'd frequently complained about meals being ruined, Katlyn couldn't argue with his logic. She'd have to wait a while before getting into his jeans.

The idea brought a sparkle to her eyes. Her expression was an enchanting mixture of mischief and provocation. "Too bad," she taunted.

"On second thought . . ." muttered Jared, narrowing the distance between them.

Katlyn effectively countered his advance by shoving a plate in his hands. "Help yourself to spaghetti and sauce."

He took the plate and gave her a look that promised retribution. It made Katlyn laugh happily. She was getting really fond of his form of reprisal and penance.

For the next half-hour, they satisfied their appetites for food and conversation. She urged Jared to tell her more about his family and the ranch's history. In the past, he'd been reluctant to talk about himself, but he seemed less wary tonight.

Katlyn wondered if he knew how much she needed the personal interaction. How starved she was to know him better. She hoped he was finally beginning to realize that her interest wasn't based on greed. She didn't think of him as a ticket to Kingston's social register. She just loved him with all her heart.

He was a complex man with deep-seated fears about commitment. She understood some of his reluctance to trust, but she wanted to know more. She wanted to know what made him wary, what made him happy, what kind of future he envisioned.

There was no doubting his deep love for his ranch and his heritage. Pride was evident in every mention of his work. Katlyn thrilled at finally being included in his discussion of the things that were most important to him.

"Do you still have a lot of strays to round up?" she asked when they were finished eating and lingering over coffee.

Jared rose from his chair and started carrying their dishes to the sink.

"We have herds farther north. We'll spend the next few days driving them closer to the ranch."

"I'm sorry I can't help," she said. "I don't have another day off until Sunday."

Jared took hold of her hand and pulled her from her chair into his arms. "Sunday's a long way off. Does that mean I won't see you 'til then?"

"You can come to the restaurant for dinner every night," she suggested, cupping his face in her hands and stroking his tense jaw with her thumbs.

Their gazes met, and Katlyn gasped as his hands clutched her bare bottom, drawing her against him. Her body, already so sensitive to his touch, prickled with a new tension.

"Or you could come sleep with me every night."

His tone bordered on a challenge that Katlyn decided to ignore. She'd told him she wouldn't live with him again. He obviously thought there was still room for negotiation.

"It's getting late, and I have to go soon. Let's not argue."

"You don't have to go. You want to go."

Katlyn didn't like the censure in his tone or the tightening of his jaw. Deciding to distract him, she reached for the snap of his cutoffs and flicked it open. Her gaze never left his as she began to explore.

He'd kept his share of the bargain. There was nothing but bare skin under the jeans. Somehow she found the nerve to stroke him. Her eyes widened as his satiny flesh swelled in her hands. It was the first time she'd ever touched him this way, and her expression revealed her awe.

"Damn, Katie."

"Like that?" Her question was a hoarse whisper. She watched his eyes dilate with desire, and her caresses grew bolder.

Jared's low groan shivered over her body, making her ache, too. In a matter of minutes they were both straining for closer contact; their desire flaring to life at the speed of light.

He fished a condom from his pocket, and she took great pleasure applying it while he shoved the cutoffs down his legs.

Then he braced himself against the counter and lifted her high enough to bury his face between her breasts. She locked her legs around his hips and accepted him into her body, luxuriating in the way he trembled with need.

Their mouths met and locked. Katlyn tasted wine and his hunger. He plunged his tongue through her lips, initiating a sexual foray that left her panting for breath.

When their passion was spent, she sagged against him, not trusting her own quivering legs for support. Their hearts pounded wildly, almost in rhythm, as they struggled to regain control.

Eventually, Jared eased her onto a chair, then briefly excused himself.

"Don't move."

Katlyn nodded in agreement. She couldn't have moved if her life depended on it. Not so Jared. He left the room, but quickly returned to clean the kitchen. He didn't bother to don his jeans again, so she watched his every move in rapt fascination.

"I hope you don't have any Peeping Toms around here."

He turned on the dishwasher, switched off the light and turned to her again. "Just in case, we'd better move upstairs."

Katlyn's brows arched. His stamina and insatiable desire amazed her. "You can't be serious?"

"Serious as hell," he said, as he scooped her into his arms and planted a hard kiss on her lips. "I suffered weeks of deprivation."

Laughter bubbled up from her chest. "And you're trying to recoup your losses all in one day?"

"That, and it's a long time 'til Sunday."

Her delighted laughter rang through the house as Jared carried her to his bedroom. She would have to leave soon. Her aunt Trudy would be home from the restaurant and worrying about her. But for the next hour or so, she just wanted more special time with the man she loved.

She could break her promise to herself and spend the night. The temptation was strong as he tumbled her into his bed, pulled the T-shirt over her head and buried his face between her breasts.

Her body went taut with tension again, but she silently vowed to withstand the temptation. Staying would be a huge mistake. And she prided herself in never making the same mistake twice.

Jared watched the glowing taillights of Katlyn's car until they blinked out of sight. It was only eleven o'clock, but she'd insisted on going home. None of his arguments had made so much as a dent in her determination to leave. She could be as stubborn as his twenty-year-old tractor.

He went back to bed, but didn't expect to sleep. Katlyn was driving him crazy. She was a fever in his blood. She'd gotten under his skin like no other woman ever had.

When they'd first met, he'd thought that living with her would sate his desire. It hadn't. He'd told himself that the emotional stress of his legal battles and the extra hours of work had made him vulnerable.

He'd even convinced himself that the reality of having her again wouldn't live up to his memories of those weeks together. He'd been wrong. He hated being wrong. Hated this steadily growing need for her.

The scent of her enveloped him as he stretched out in bed. A cool breeze blew in the window. He welcomed the chill, but it didn't temper the heat of his thoughts.

This new arrangement was better than nothing, but not nearly what he wanted. He didn't like sharing Katlyn with that restaurant or her many friends and customers. He didn't like the idea that another man could come along and offer her more than he was willing to offer.

Obsession. The word popped into his head again. He didn't like it, but he couldn't deny it. He was obsessed with Katlyn. She refused to live with him, and he didn't think she'd change her mind. The only other solution would be to marry her.

Marriage. He'd sworn never to give any woman the means or opportunity to claim King property. His grandfather had fought to keep his grandmother from depleting precious assets. His father had relived the battle with his mother. Even his stepmother had tried to take a chunk of his heritage.

The King men were notoriously poor judges of character when it came to the opposite sex. Hormones had always overridden common sense. He'd vowed not to be another victim.

Could he trust Katlyn? Was she sincere, or just more subtle than the other women who'd tried to trap him over the years? There had been too many. Woman who professed their love, but had really yearned for his money.

She'd sworn she loved him, had told him often during those first weeks together. He hadn't wanted to hear the words then, but he'd expected her to repeat them today. She hadn't. He should be relieved. He wasn't. And that bothered him even more.

Maybe she realized that all they had going was a strong case of lust. Maybe she'd decided that all she wanted was a part-time lover. Or maybe she was holding out for a wedding ring.

She hadn't mentioned marriage today, either. Had she changed her mind about that, too? He had to wonder what she'd say if he proposed.

Would she say yes to a prenuptial agreement? They could both sign a document that would protect their separate interests. He didn't want her restaurant, so maybe she really didn't want a claim on his property.

The idea of any long-term commitment was worrisome. In his experience, the physical passion waned after a few months. What did you do with a wife then? His grandfather and father had chosen divorce. He would never even consider it.

And what if Katlyn wanted children? She'd lost most of her family at an early age. Would she want to create a whole new one?

There'd been a time when he'd savored the idea, but not anymore. . . .

Eight

Katlyn leaned over the toilet bowl, so sick she felt like her stomach was about to turn inside out. This was the third morning in a row she'd had the dry heaves the minute she got out of bed.

At first, she'd thought it might be caused by too much sun exposure last Wednesday. Or that it might have been a result of too much emotional trauma. She'd run out of plausible excuses, but there was no avoiding the facts any longer.

She was definitely experiencing symptoms of early pregnancy: Morning sickness. Uncharacteristic bouts of tears. Falling asleep at the drop of a hat.

Her mind raced as she bathed her face and brushed her teeth. She couldn't delay any longer. She'd have to go out of town to buy one of those in-home test kits. Most of Kingston would know within hours if she made that kind of purchase locally.

After getting dressed and eating a light breakfast, she made the hour-long trip to the nearest shopping center. She spent a few hours browsing for clothes, but returned home in time for her evening shift at the restaurant.

Business was brisk, as usual, but she did as much soul-searching as she did cooking. What if she was carrying Jared's child? What would she do? How would she tell him?

Trudy would insist that they get married. Jared probably would, too, but he'd hate it. He'd feel trapped, betrayed and resentful. Even if he was equally responsible for the pregnancy, he'd feel like a victim.

Both his grandfather and father had married under similar circumstances. Both marriages had been disasters, scarring Jared at an early age with their bitterness.

Katlyn's heart ached every time she thought about their special day together. She wanted so much from their relationship. They'd taken giant steps toward emotional as well as physical intimacy. Now that growing trust would be shattered.

Worried and distracted, the evening seemed to drag on forever. Jared didn't make it to the restaurant to eat. She was relieved, yet felt guilty for feeling that way. She missed him and badly wanted to see him, but was afraid he might see a difference in her: A difference she hadn't quite come to terms with yet.

Begging off from the usual Saturday evening poker game, Katlyn headed home as soon as the restaurant closed. But the minute she entered the house, the phone started ringing.

"Hello."

"Hello to you."

As always, the sound of Jared's voice melted something deep inside of her. She sat down in a nearby chair and hugged the phone to her ear.

"I thought you might be at the restaurant for dinner tonight," she said.

"I thought so, too, but I just got in from the barns. It's been a long day."

"And a long week." She'd talked to him each night, but hadn't actually seen him.

"Miss me?" he asked.

She didn't bother with half-truths. "A bunch."

His deep, satisfied chuckle was a reward for her honesty. "No poker game tonight?" he asked.

"I wasn't in the mood."

"Tired?"

"Dragging."

"You said tomorrow's your day off. Why don't you come spend the night with me?"

His sexy invitation sent a thrill through her. She wanted to be with him as much as he wanted her to. But she had to do the pregnancy test first thing in the morning. Spending the night was out of the question.

"I'm pretty bushed tonight."

"I'll come get you if you're too tired to drive."

"It's not that." She searched for excuses. "I still haven't had a shower. I'd rather get a good night's sleep here at home, then come out there first thing in the morning."

Katlyn could tell by the long silence that Jared didn't totally believe her reasons for not coming, and that her reluctance bothered him. It was a relief when he didn't press the issue.

"Because your aunt wouldn't approve of you spending the night?" he suggested, his tone altering slightly.

She hated laying the blame on Trudy, but gratefully accepted the out. "It would be a little more respectable if I wait."

"Respect isn't a very good bedfellow."

How well she knew! Katlyn changed the subject. "Have you missed me a little bit, too?"

"I wouldn't miss you at all if you'd move back in with me."

She closed her eyes and sighed. He thought he wanted her to live with him, but if they were forced to marry, he'd quickly learn to hate the sight of her. The thought made her stomach churn.

"If we lived together very long, you'd change your mind about that," she insisted.

"How do you figure? I didn't get tired of having you here the last time."

"Because I didn't stay very long, and I was at your beck and call every minute," she reminded. "I can't afford that sort of luxury on a long-term basis. If I moved back, I'd still want to work. Our schedules would be crazy, I'd get tired and cranky, and you'd be ready to throw me out in a couple months."

"Now that the lawsuit is settled, I can afford a little luxury. I'll hire a housekeeper. Can't you find someone to take over some of your hours at the restaurant?"

"We've been trying to hire another chef, but not too many city folk want to move to Kingston."

"You've given it some thought?" he asked.

"Some."

"Because you're willing to spend more time out here?"

She paused before answering. "We'd just get on each other's nerves."

"We did just fine on Wednesday. We worked, we ate, we made love. No strings attached. If we get tired of each other, you could always move out again."

There were always strings attached. Always a price to pay for such blissful happiness. Katlyn knew it couldn't last.

"Well, Aunt Trudy might not be too pleased to have me moving in and out on a regular basis. She's been great, but I wouldn't do that to her again."

They were quiet for a few seconds, each lost in thought. Then Jared asked, "What time can you make it out here tomorrow?"

Katlyn tried to lighten the mood. "Not six A.M.," she teased.

"Six-thirty?"

"Not even."

"Seven?"

"Maybe eight-thirty or nine."

"I'll cook breakfast. If you're not here by nine, I'll eat it all myself."

Breakfast hadn't been her favorite meal of late, but she accepted the offer. "It's a date."

A yawn escaped, and Katlyn apologized. "I guess I'd better say good night before I fall asleep in this chair."

"You're not in bed yet?"

"Nope. Are you?"

"No, but I will be in a couple minutes."

She closed her eyes and pictured him in his bedroom, showered and ready for bed. The mental image made her yearn for closer contact. The need to be near him, see him, touch him was overwhelming. She wanted the comfort of emotional as well as physical intimacy.

Katlyn realized that the stress of the last few days

was taking its toll on her. Still, she wished she felt confident enough in their relationship to share her worries with Jared. She wanted to tell him she loved him and hear him say the same without hesitation. She wanted him to assure her that everything would be fine.

"Are you falling asleep?"

Her reply was soft; her voice a little shaky. "No, but I'd better say good night before I do."

"Katlyn?"

The concern in his tone made her feel even more weepy. "I'll see you tomorrow. Bye now," she whispered before he could ask any more questions.

First thing out of bed the next morning, Katlyn was sick again. And the pregnancy test was positive. For a long time, she just sat and stared at the little test stick, torn between the jubilation of carrying Jared's baby and concerns about the future.

A good night's sleep had restored her self-confidence. Regardless of anyone else's reaction to the pregnancy, she desperately wanted this child. She wanted a family of her own and was prepared to take full responsibility for this new life.

She'd considered all the angles over the past few days, and had decided not to tell Jared right away. She needed time to come to terms with the fact herself. Besides, he might insist she marry him, which she'd have to refuse. Even worse, he might turn against her and sue for custody of their child.

She had no problem with giving their child his name or joint custody, but he probably wouldn't settle for that. He had way too much clout in Kingston. If he tried to take their child, he might win. She hoped it wouldn't come to that, but she had to do everything possible to reduce the risk.

Pressing a hand to her abdomen, Katlyn stroked it gently. She was going to be a mother and she refused to allow anyone to threaten her relationship with her child.

Would it be a boy or a girl? Could she carry it to term without any problems? She was healthy, so the baby should be healthy, too. Taking good care of herself should ensure her child's health, shouldn't it?

The direction of her life was irreversibly altering, but she didn't fear or resent the change. She had a wealth of love to share and would welcome this new little person with joy.

There was no telling how Jared would feel. Responsible, yes, he was that sort of man. But could he give his unconditional love to an unplanned child? Would he hate her and himself for not preventing the conception?

She was perfectly capable of raising their child alone, but it couldn't be in Kingston. Small towns were notoriously cruel to children born out of wedlock. She'd never subject hers to that kind of ridicule and name-calling.

Perhaps it would be best to move back to the city where people tended to mind their own business and were less likely to pass judgment on her actions.

Her former instructor at the Napa Valley Culinary School had extended an open invitation for a teaching position. She'd decided the best thing to do would be to return to the city until it was absolutely necessary to tell Jared. By then, she'd be well established in her work and it would be harder for him to challenge her decision.

But how in the world was she going to explain the sudden move without telling either Trudy or Jared the whole truth?

Katlyn returned to her bedroom and was racking her brain for ideas when her aunt tapped on the door, then stuck her head in the room.

"I was just checking to see if you wanted to go to church with me," said Trudy.

"Not today, thanks. Jared invited me out to his house for breakfast."

A worried frown creased the older woman's brow as she stepped further into the room. "How are things between the two of you?"

"Getting a little too intense again," Katlyn confessed, plopping down on her bed. "I've been thinking about going away for a while."

"Where would you go?" her aunt asked.

"I've been thinking about visiting Napa Valley. That way I could do a little recruiting while I'm gone. It would leave you short of help until I can find a replacement."

"I'm not concerned about the restaurant," said Trudy. "We'll get by somehow. I can cook, and Donna's learning. I'm worried about you. Do you think leaving for a couple weeks will really make a difference in the way Jared feels?"

Katlyn plucked at the bedspread. "Actually, I've been considering a more permanent move, but I'll have to see if there's a place for me out there first."

"Permanent," Trudy repeated softly. "Have you told Jared yet?"

For a moment, all Katlyn could do was stare at her aunt. She thought Trudy was asking her if she'd told him about the baby, then she realized her aunt was talking about her relocation.

Embarrassed, she quickly covered her reaction. "I haven't mentioned it yet. He's not going to be pleased, but we can't go on this way forever. We just want totally different things from our relationship."

"Do you really think that putting some distance between you will help?" asked Trudy. Her expression was compassionate and understanding. "It won't make you love him any less."

Katlyn gave her a sad smile. "Nothing's going to change the way I feel, but he doesn't want my love."

"Nonsense. He needs a good woman more than any man I've ever met. And he cares deeply for you. He's just too stubborn to admit it, even to himself."

"I don't want a man who just needs me. If I ever marry, it will be to a man who both needs me and can love me every bit as much as I love him. If that's not possible, then I'll be just fine by myself."

Trudy didn't argue. "How soon were you planning to leave?"

"As soon as we can make arrangements. Within the next two weeks, if possible."

"You were terribly homesick when you lived out there before," her aunt reminded.

Katlyn hadn't forgotten. She'd be even more homesick this time because of Jared, but now she had another life to consider. She'd soon be too busy to worry about homesickness.

"I'll miss everyone, but if I take a teaching position, I'll be busy. I might even get a part-time cooking job until I can get established."

"Well, you haven't touched your share of the restaurant profits."

Katlyn was thankful she didn't have to worry about money. The restaurant was providing a healthy income, and she had savings. That could all change quickly, though, if she ran into problems with her pregnancy.

"I'm not too worried about finances. We might even consider opening a franchise in California. I can be on the lookout for locations. You'd love the weather, especially in the winter."

"I'm sure I would." Trudy smiled encouragingly, although they both knew she'd never willingly leave Kingston. "Are you planning to tell Jared today? He's not going to be pleased, you know. He'll try to dissuade you."

Katlyn was well aware of the battle ahead of her. She'd have to convince Jared and herself that they needed to break things off.

He wouldn't like it, but it was his fault for having so little faith in their relationship. He'd had ample opportunity to make things right between them. Now he'd just have to accept her decision, like it or not.

Trudy chuckled, regaining her attention. "You're wearing that expression you used to get when you were little. You always hated having someone tell you that you couldn't do something you really wanted to do."

Katlyn forced a smile. "I guess I can be every bit as obstinate as he can."

The older woman turned to leave, laughing outright. "I don't doubt it one bit, honey. Since you're going out to the ranch, I probably won't come home right after church. Have a nice day, and don't let Jared bully you."

Katlyn said goodbye and glanced at the clock. She was due at his house in less than half an hour. She wasn't worried about him trying to bully her. He'd want to make love.

She wanted that, too. She wanted more memories to take with her when she left home, but it wouldn't be right. It wasn't fair to continue seeing him now that she'd decided to end it. How could she lie in his arms and lie to them both? It would make a mockery of her love for him.

The only decent thing to do would be to break it off right now. Now that she'd decided to leave, she couldn't risk having him find out about the baby. At least until she could put hundreds of miles between them.

What if she got sick at his house? Or fainted? Pregnant women always did that in the movies. Shocked, Katlyn stared at the familiar surroundings of her childhood bedroom, and found something more to worry about. What if their loving earlier in the week had hurt the baby?

She didn't know anything about pregnancy. Could they have done something wrong? They'd been so passionate and insatiable. They'd even made love standing up in the kitchen. The memory sent a surge of heat through her body.

She'd had a glass of wine, too. Wasn't that dangerous to the baby's health? And the horseback riding. Could that be harmful to the baby? Dear heaven, what if she'd already done something that might hurt their child?

How was a person supposed to know these things?

She had to get to a doctor as soon as possible. It would have to be in California, not Wyoming. She would need a prenatal exam and information and vitamins and someone to answer all the questions!

Picking up the phone, she dialed Jared's number, bracing herself for a less than pleasant conversation.

How was she going to explain that she didn't want to continue their relationship? Especially after the day of loving they'd shared earlier in the week. He was bound to think she was playing games. He'd accuse her of trying to manipulate him again.

She'd begun to hope their relationship had a chance, but the pregnancy changed that. Even if he knew and was willing to offer marriage, she couldn't accept. It would be like marrying with two strikes against them—unfair to everyone involved.

"King."

"Jared, it's Katlyn."

"Hey, sweetheart, breakfast is almost ready. You'd better hightail it out here or I'll eat it all myself."

Katlyn closed her eyes. Her chest tightened and a lump lodged in her throat. The endearment was so rare that she added it to the treasured memories. He sounded so relaxed and cheerful.

Usually, he worked too hard and played too little. She dreaded having to dampen his high spirits.

"I think I'm going to have to take a rain check," she managed after clearing her throat.

His tone abruptly echoed concern. "What's wrong? You sound upset. Is it Trudy?"

"No, no, nothing's wrong," she lied. "Trudy's fine. She's going to church, but told me to say hello for her."

"Then what's the problem? Are you sick?"

Sick at heart, thought Katlyn. Bolstering her courage, she braved his wrath. "I'm not sick, just having some doubts about us again."

He swore, his tone growing rough. "What the hell's going on, Katlyn? You didn't have any doubts earlier in the week. Or even last night."

Her whole life had changed since Wednesday; since she'd seen the positive color of that little test stick. She couldn't explain, so her excuse sounded especially lame.

"I'm sorry, I thought I was sophisticated enough to just enjoy having an affair, but I guess I'm not."

There was a long, tense silence. She knew Jared was battling to control his temper. He was going to hate her for blowing hot and cold.

"What the hell does sophistication have to do with anything?" he finally demanded. "You either want to be with me or you don't. It's that simple."

It had never been that simple for her, only him. That was where they really differed. She was glad she'd decided not to tell him about the baby yet. Time and distance would surely add a new perspective.

"Then maybe I just don't want to be with you badly enough." Katlyn managed to choke out another lie.

The sound of Jared's harshly indrawn breath stabbed at her conscience. Would the rejection wound his heart or just his pride and ego?

"Are you telling me that you didn't enjoy our time together? That all your passionate responses were faked? That you have no desire to be with me again?"

Those ridiculous, annoying tears were streaming

down her face again and clogging her throat. She covered the receiver while she cleared her voice. This was dangerous ground, so she chose her words very carefully.

"I'm not saying I didn't enjoy our time together. You're a wonderful lover." Just remembering gave her a secret thrill. She paused to regroup.

"But?" Jared challenged.

But what? She had no idea how to answer. He was demanding details, and there were none. She'd loved every second of time they'd spent together, yet she had to come up with a plausible explanation for her reluctance.

"But I've decided that I'm just not woman enough for you."

It was such a sorry excuse that her stomach rolled again. She could visualize Jared's expression of disbelief. His dark eyes would be sparkling with anger, his mouth set in a grim line.

"Is that supposed to be a joke?" he all but snarled. "It's not funny. Maybe you'd better try telling me the truth."

He wasn't falling for her line. Katlyn bit her lip. What now? How could she possibly convince him that she wanted to end their relationship?

"Better yet," Jared snapped, "I'll come over and you can tell me to my face."

Panic surged through Katlyn. She couldn't face him right now. She felt too confused and vulnerable.

"No! You can't come here. I don't want to see you!" she insisted, her distress evident.

Jared's tone grew suspicious. "Is someone with

you?" Then his voice deepened to a lethal intensity. "Are you calling from someone else's house?"

"N-no," she stuttered. The question caught her off guard. What was he implying? That she had spent the night with someone else? Did he really believe her capable of such duplicity? So much for her attempts to earn his trust.

Abruptly, her guilt changed to irritation, halting her tears and adding a little acid to her tone. "I'm at home. Trudy's still in the house, but nobody else is here. How could you even suggest such a thing?"

"Why wouldn't I? Something must have prompted your call."

"So you automatically mistrust me?" she wanted to know. Annoyance offered the first real outlet she'd had for too much conflicting emotion. "What sort of woman jumps from one man's bed to another?"

"You tell me."

His cool, detached question really fired Katlyn's anger. Her voice grew shrill. "You're hopeless! Do you hear me, Jared? Hopeless! I'm not coming to your house because I'm tired of trying to convince you that I can be trusted. You're the only person I've ever met in my whole life who doubted my integrity, insulted my motives and accused me of unspeakable things!"

She was on a roll and unleashed the full force of her frustration on him. "I'm tired of it. That's why I'm not coming out there today or ever again. We're finished. Period. Just like you said. No strings attached. Right? Abso-damn-lutely no strings!"

Katlyn slammed down the phone, then knocked

it back off the hook. If he tried to call her, he could listen to the stupid busy signal.

Her stomach threatened to erupt, and she headed to the bathroom, alternately cursing and crying.

Nine

Jared stared at the phone, stunned by Katlyn's display of temper. What in the world was wrong with her? She couldn't possibly have meant any of that.

"Hey, boss, sure smells good in here," Dan said as he entered the house through the back porch.

"I cooked breakfast. Help yourself," he replied, hanging up the phone.

"Expecting company?" asked the foreman as he grabbed a slice of bacon.

"Katlyn was supposed to come out, but she just called and canceled. Then she got mad, started yelling and hung up on me."

He dialed her number, but got a busy signal. Frowning, he replaced the receiver. "Now she's left the phone off the hook."

"What'd she get so mad about?"

"Hell if I know. She just keeps blowing hot and cold. It's driving me nuts. Women!"

"Yeah," the other man agreed, leaning against the counter and munching bacon. "When a woman's hot, she can set your blood on fire. But when she's cold . . . brrrrrrrr."

Jared raked a hand through his hair in frustration, then started clearing up his mess.

"I don't know what's gotten into her. She was

never this way when she lived here. Last night she was all sweet and lonesome. This morning she's grumpy as a bear and never wants to see me again."

"Maybe it's just a monthly thing."

Jared considered the possibility, then shook his head. "She never got that moody before, even when she felt really bad."

He didn't notice that his foreman had gone still and thoughtful. "Does she break into tears at the drop of a hat?"

Jared thought about their conversation on the phone last night. He would have sworn there were tears in her voice.

"Yeah."

"How about sleepy? Has she been tired a lot lately? Yawnin' all the time and takin' a lot of cat-naps?"

Another memory surfaced. Katlyn curled up in his bed. She'd fallen asleep a few times on Wednesday, but she'd had good reason to be tired.

"Maybe she's just working too many hours. I guess it could be stress."

"Maybe," drawled Dan. "On the other hand, my Mary's a pretty even-tempered woman. A lot like your Katlyn. I can only remember her being that tired, grumpy and weepy three times in fifteen years of marriage."

"Three times?"

"Yeah. When she was pregnant."

An abrupt silence fell between them as Jared stared at his friend. "Pregnant?" he repeated, dazed by the thought. "But we . . ."

"Always used protection," Dan finished his sentence. "How many kids you think got their start in the world because their parents believed that?"

A chill raced down Jared's spine. "Why would you even think it? Have you heard gossip?"

"Nope, just Mary's intuition. She didn't figure Katlyn was on birth control when she moved in with you, and it takes a while for those pills to be effective. The odds aren't as good with other methods."

Jared didn't argue with the facts, but suddenly Katlyn's behavior seemed more chilling. She'd said they were finished. No strings. She wouldn't have said that if she was pregnant. She and her aunt would probably be demanding a wedding.

He shook his head sharply, dismissing the idea. "She'd have told me about a baby."

"Would she?" Dan helped himself to more bacon. "She strikes me as a pretty independent lady, and you've made it clear about not wantin' to be tied down."

"She's the one who wanted marriage. Do you really think she'd pass up an opportunity like that?"

"Maybe, maybe not. Every time I try to figure out what makes women tick, I get it ass-backward."

Expression grim, Jared headed for the door. "I'm going to town."

"I'll take care of things here," Dan promised, a slow grin creasing his weathered face.

Jared didn't notice. He strode to his truck, climbed in and revved the engine. The tires squealed as he stomped on the accelerator. His mind raced as he drove the ten miles to town in record time.

Pregnant. No, she couldn't be. A pregnancy would have Katlyn acting just the opposite. She'd be making demands instead of telling him they were finished.

No strings attached. Her words echoed in his ears, making his insides churn. They were his words, but he'd never expected to have them thrown in his face. It forced him to accept the fact that he didn't want a relationship with abso-damn-lutely no strings. He wanted Katlyn bound to him.

There had to be some other reason for her erratic behavior. Maybe she was torn between loyalties to her aunt and to him. Maybe he'd pressured her too much. Or maybe she really didn't want to be with him. That thought bothered him more than he cared to admit.

Maybe his unappeasable desire for her was a problem. She'd always met his passion with equal fervor, but he supposed she could have been faking it. It wouldn't be the first time a woman had pulled the wool over his eyes.

There was always a chance that Ryan Havens was at the root of the problem, too. Maybe Katlyn had finally decided to accept whatever the other man was offering. Jared felt a jolt of hot emotion at the thought. His hands tightened on the steering wheel.

He slowed the truck as he approached the edge of town and caught sight of Katlyn's house. In another few minutes, he was parked in her driveway and swinging out of the truck.

Trudy opened the door just as he reached the porch. She looked surprised to see him, but offered a friendly smile.

"Good morning, Jared. I thought Katlyn was coming out to your place for breakfast."

He managed to keep his tone level. "Change of plans."

"Well, I'm on my way to church and running a little late." She stepped aside, leaving the door open. "Katlyn's still in her room, so just go on in and yell for her. I'll see you both later."

Jared told her goodbye and moved into the house. When a call to Katlyn didn't get a response, he closed the door, crossed the living room and climbed the stairs to the second floor.

There were only three doors. He knocked on the one that was closed, then shoved it open and stepped inside. Katlyn's sweet, familiar scent enveloped him, tightening his gut.

The shower shut off in her bath, explaining why she hadn't heard him calling. Deciding to wait until she finished in the bathroom, he walked further into the room.

The morning sun poured in two long windows, illuminating the multicolored, very feminine decor. The bed was still rumpled, and Katlyn's thin lavender nightgown was tossed across the end of it. The intimacy of it tightened his chest.

Shaken by his reaction to her private domain, Jared walked to one of the windows and looked out. He used the next few minutes to calm the adrenaline pumping through his veins. He didn't turn until he heard the bathroom door open.

Katlyn appeared, wearing a short, white terry robe. She was securing a towel around her wet hair when she caught sight of him and stopped abruptly.

"Jared!"

She looked incredibly soft and vulnerable at first glance. Her face was flushed pink and the white robe gave her a look of virginal innocence. The muscles in his arms contracted with the urge to hold her, but he forced himself not to react.

Then her expression changed. The result wasn't welcoming. He watched her eyes narrow warily, and her stance grow defensive. Both telling actions annoyed him.

"Why are you here?" she demanded. "Don't tell me you came just to see if I was telling the truth. I'm not entertaining other men in my bedroom."

His earlier accusation had been prompted by an insane flash of jealousy. He hadn't really thought she was sharing a bed with anyone else, and he didn't like letting his emotions get out of hand.

"That remark was way out of line. I apologize."

His apology took her by surprise. He could see it in her eyes. But instead of making her relax, it seemed to make her more wary.

"I have to wonder if you're apologizing because it's obvious you were wrong, or because you're really sorry for doubting me in the first place."

Jared didn't see much use in responding. He knew she wouldn't believe him, and that's what really bothered him. He couldn't make any sense of her attitude. Why was she suddenly so defensive?

Did she really want him out of her life? Was it because of Havens? Or was it possible Dan had supplied the right answer? His gaze dropped to her stomach.

"We need to talk."

A blush crept up Katlyn's neck and face. She turned slightly and pulled the towel from her head, efforts he knew were meant to distract his attention.

"Not in here," she protested. "If you want to go

downstairs, I'll be down as soon as I get dressed and dry my hair."

What he wanted was her mouth; some physical connection to counteract the chilling emotional distance. The need was too intense, too overpowering to ignore, and he reached her in two steps.

She froze like a startled deer as he took the towel from her unresisting grip and pitched it aside. Then he sank his fingers in her damp, silky locks, tilting her head up as he brought his down.

Her lips opened on a gasp of surprise, and he slid his tongue deep into the warmth of her mouth. He savored the sweet, moist contact.

Her hands flew to his chest. Not to caress, but as a barrier to keep some distance between them. The action shook him, and he fought the urge to shatter her resistance.

Instead, he made love to her mouth, caressing the soft insides of her cheeks with slow, gentle strokes of his tongue. Then he teased her tongue until he'd coaxed it into his mouth where he sucked greedily.

His hands tightened on her head as she began to respond. He felt some of the tension leaving her body as her fingers curled into his chest, no longer holding him at bay.

A shudder of relief coursed through him. Their response to each other hadn't diminished in intensity. The attraction was still strong, and that gave him the edge to deal with whatever else was bothering her.

"I'll wait downstairs," he whispered against her mouth as he slowly broke off the kiss. Then he let go of her head, turned and left the room.

Katlyn was so shaken by his kiss that her legs were trembling. She took a few steps to her bed and sat down heavily. Lifting a hand to her mouth, she touched her lips and groaned.

Damn him. Damn him for so quickly and tenderly destroying her defenses.

If he'd tried to overpower her physically, she'd have punched him. If he'd taken her in his arms, she'd have quickly put him in his place. But no. He hadn't tried to control her with his strength. He'd seduced her with tenderness. And he'd done it so well.

To add to her confusion was the impression that he'd badly needed that kiss. Needed it with a deep emotional hunger he'd probably never admit. It was a humbling thought that created a surge of hope.

She quickly subdued her wayward thoughts. She couldn't allow them to drift in that direction. Jared's needs and wants were no longer her main concern. She had too many other worries at the moment.

Swiping the foolish tears from her cheeks, Katlyn tried to stir the flames of anger she'd felt earlier. Had he come here just to make a liar out of her? To prove that there was still a strong attraction between them?

Why else would he have come? Katlyn asked herself the question as she rose from the bed and pulled a sweat suit from her dresser drawer. Then she chastised herself for wondering.

It didn't matter why Jared was here. What mattered was convincing him that they were finished. And telling him that she was moving out of state, plus making sure he understood there was nothing he could do to stop her.

Her sweat suit was old, the bright turquoise faded to a paler shade, but it was comfortable. The weather had turned cool and it was warm. Once Katlyn was dressed and had her hair dried, she felt better prepared to face Jared.

She found him in the kitchen. Trudy had left coffee warming and a plate of sweet rolls on the table. He had helped himself to both.

"Hope you don't mind."

Katlyn shook her head. Neither of them mentioned the fact that he'd already cooked one breakfast this morning.

She poured herself a big glass of milk and joined him at the table. Sweet rolls weren't the most nutritious meal, but she was too hungry to care. Between them, they finished the entire plateful.

Once their hunger was satisfied, the silence grew more pronounced. Katlyn poured herself some coffee and refilled Jared's cup. His gaze never left her as she moved around the kitchen and then sat back down. She supposed there was no sense in delaying any longer.

"I've decided to go away for a while." She didn't look directly at Jared, but sensed the impact her words had on him.

"Why?"

That one word in his tightly controlled tone scared her more than any tirade from him. Katlyn felt her own tension increase, but she managed to look him in the eyes.

"I'm just not very happy with my life right now. I've decided it's time for a change."

"Is this the I-need-to-find-myself routine?" he asked grimly. "Or the tried and true I-need-some-space?"

Katlyn dropped her gaze. "A little of both, I guess."

"You've made plans?"

Her plans were so tentative that she dodged a direct answer. "I thought I'd visit the culinary school in Napa Valley. That way I can do a little on-site recruiting."

"California," he said. "That's a helluva long way to go to think. How long will you be away?"

She wasn't ready to tell him the move would be permanent, and she didn't want to lie. "I really don't know."

"A week? A month?" he challenged. "I thought you had responsibilities at the restaurant. Doesn't Trudy need to know how long you'll be gone?"

"She assured me it won't be a problem. I guess I'm not so indispensable after all."

Her attempt to lighten the tension fell flat, and she knew that dodging his questions made her actions seem more suspect. She didn't want to spur his curiosity, but was at a loss for reasonable explanations.

For another long, silent minute they sipped their coffee and stared at each other. Then Jared totally shattered the silence.

"Dan thinks you're pregnant."

Katlyn's breath hissed out in a gasp. She dropped her cup and spilled the rest of her coffee. Jumping out of her chair, she reached for a dishcloth to mop the dark liquid from the tabletop.

Jared rose too, clearing the dishes out of her way

and taking them to the sink. They quickly cleaned up the spill, then Katlyn stalled for time as she rinsed the cloth and the dishes.

The silence grew ominous, but she felt totally inadequate. She couldn't look at him, couldn't formulate a response, couldn't bring herself to deny she was carrying his child.

Jared didn't allow her any slack. He cupped her face in his hand, forcing her to look at him.

"Are you pregnant?"

Katlyn's throat went dry. She didn't want to say the words that might immediately transform them from lovers to enemies.

"Katlyn?" he prodded.

"I think so."

"Think?" he asked sharply, eyes narrowing.

"It hasn't been confirmed by a doctor, but the early pregnancy test was positive," she admitted, pulling free of his grip.

She poured herself another cup of coffee, not really wanting it, but needing something to do.

"Is it mine?"

The anger that surged through her was so fierce and hot that it caught her off guard. In an instant, she was trembling with the force of her fury. When she was finally able to reply, it was with tightly leashed control.

"I guess that answers my earlier question. Your apology obviously meant nothing. You really do believe I'm capable of bed hopping, don't you?"

Jared shrugged off the question and asked another. "How stupid would I be if I didn't ask?"

Katlyn clamped her teeth shut and just stared at

him. He was serious. It was in his eyes. He really
didn't know why she should object to his question.

"I don't suppose the word *trust* means anything
to you, does it? You might consider trusting me
enough to know I wouldn't have sex with someone
else while we're having a sexual relationship!"

"Sex and trust don't necessarily go hand in
hand," he snapped.

"No." She snapped right back at him, venting a
little of her fury. "Trust can stand all by itself. Without sex. Even without love. Trust is based on having
faith in someone's honor and integrity. It's about
morals and believing in someone besides yourself."

They glared at each other for one long minute,
then Jared responded, "All right. You've made your
point." Raking a hand through his hair, he began
to pace. "When is the baby due?"

Katlyn took a seat at the table again when all the
strength in her legs deserted her. She forced herself
to breathe deeply and regain some calm.

"Sometime in May, I think. I told you I haven't
seen a doctor."

"Do you have an appointment? Dr. Stoneridge is
still practicing in Kingston."

"I'm not seeing old Dr. Stoneridge or anyone else
around here," she declared mutinously. "I'll find a
good OB/GYN in Napa Valley."

He stopped pacing and stared at her. "The hell
you will. What's wrong with seeing someone right
here? Or someone in Casper?"

"You're asking me? The whole town would know
within minutes. I won't do that to Aunt Trudy, the
baby or myself. I've given the gossips enough scan-

dal to feed on this year. I'm not going through it all over again."

"How the hell do you plan to avoid talk? If you're expecting a baby, then there's no stopping it."

"There is if I'm not living here. Everyone will eventually learn the truth, but I'm not planning to flaunt my condition or subject an illegitimate child to their scrutiny."

"Illegitimate?"

"That's what they call children born out of wedlock, you know. Illegitimate."

"Bastards," Jared supplied fiercely. "You don't think I'm letting a child of mine be labeled a bastard, do you? We'll get married as soon as a doctor confirms the pregnancy."

He couldn't have hurt her worse if he'd stabbed her with a knife. Katlyn clamped her mouth shut and fought back a sob. Not only did he arrogantly assume she'd want marriage, but he wanted a doctor's confirmation before trusting her word.

The silence had grown heavy again before she managed to control her emotions enough to reply.

"I'm not going to a local doctor, and I'm not marrying you. I'm going to California. I'll see a doctor there and keep you advised."

Her cool, dismissive tone hit him with a biting force. She saw the look of stunned disbelief cross his face, but felt no remorse. Jared King was an arrogant, spoiled, hardheaded idiot, and she was tired of trying to convert him to humanity.

"Keep me advised?" he repeated in a dangerously soft tone.

He was livid. She could see it in every line of his body. His eyes blazed with it, but Katlyn didn't so much as flinch. She looked him straight in the eyes and stated her case.

"The only thing we can be one hundred percent sure of is that if I'm pregnant, the baby is mine. I plan to do what I think is best for both of us."

"Like marrying the father. In other words, marrying me."

It had taken long enough, but he finally admitted to his share of responsibility. The small concession pleased Katlyn, but didn't change her tune.

"No, I will not marry you. You've made it very clear that you want nothing to do with marriage or a family. I refuse to commit myself to a lifetime of that sort of attitude. I won't be the wife of a man who resents me and our child."

The atmosphere in the kitchen cracked with tension. Every bit of it was evident in Jared's tone when he finally spoke again.

"You think you're holding all the cards, huh? You think you have all the answers?"

"That's right. I'm in control of my life and plan to keep it that way. I won't allow you to demoralize me and add me to your list of wicked women who trapped the great King men into marriage."

"I never accused you of trying to trap me."

"Believe me, if we got married, that's all I'd hear for the rest of my life. Your attitude and behavior would be echoed throughout the community. I won't have it. I'm leaving."

"Running away!"

"I think of it as finding a better place to raise my child."

"And you think I'll just let you move out of state without a fight?"

Katlyn's hand trembled, betraying the fact that she wasn't as confident as she sounded. As quickly as her anger had appeared, it dissipated, leaving her feeling drained and vulnerable again.

She'd known Jared would fight her once he learned the truth. She just wasn't sure to what extent he was willing to fight. The possibilities scared her. Her only hope was that he'd grown so sick of legal battles that he'd be willing to keep their fight out of the courts.

"I promise not to be unreasonable about visitation and that sort of thing."

It was a lame promise, at best. She dared to look directly at Jared. His fists clenched at his sides, and his whole body was rigid with tension. He practically radiated anger and frustration as her words registered.

"The only promise I want from you is that you won't leave Kingston until we've both had more time to talk this out."

Katlyn wasn't sure how much more talking she could handle. Their arguing had already drained her energy. She was about as strong as a rag doll. She just wanted to be alone for a while.

"I promise I won't try to sneak out of town or anything equally juvenile."

Jared stepped close to her. Close enough that she had to tip her head slightly to meet his eyes. Close enough that she could feel the effects of his heat and scent on her equilibrium.

"How about one more promise?" he asked.

Warily, and with a tight throat, she managed to ask, "What?"

"Promise me you'll come out to the ranch for supper. I'll cook, and we can talk."

Katlyn searched his expression for some clue to his feelings, but found none. Heat warmed her cheeks as she dropped her gaze to the table.

"I won't sleep with you. That's not the answer," she insisted.

"You promise to come out and you have my promise I won't touch you. I'm not planning a seduction."

Katlyn looked at him again. Could she trust him to keep his word? *Yes.* The answer came in a heartbeat. She trusted him implicitly. He didn't trust her, so the feeling was completely one-sided. Probably because her love was equally one-sided.

"What time?"

She could have sworn Jared was holding his breath until she answered. His reply came in a relieved rush.

"I should be done with chores by six. Any time after that."

"Okay."

"Promise?" he wanted assurances.

"My promise doesn't really mean anything unless you trust me, Jared."

"I told Dan that I trusted you to tell me if you were pregnant. Apparently you don't think it's a two-way street."

Katlyn wasn't accepting that guilt trip. "I just found out this morning, and I told you already."

"But you didn't want to."

No, she hadn't wanted to. At least not so soon. He brought home the point that her trust had limitations. She trusted his word. He was an honorable man. But she didn't trust him with her heart . . . or her future.

Ten

Katlyn approached Jared's house later that evening with a confusing mix of anticipation and trepidation. She longed to be near him, yet her love was so intense that it fueled her determination to leave Kingston. She loved him far too much to marry him if he couldn't return her love.

More arguments were inevitable, and her fragile emotional state made her so vulnerable right now. She needed all the stamina she could muster for those arguments. Especially as she fully intended to win any dispute over the baby's future.

Convinced that there was absolutely nothing Jared could do to change her mind, she parked her car and walked to the door. She'd foregone her usual jeans and shirt for an aqua silk pantsuit that always made her feel good. The chic outfit offered a much-needed boost to her confidence.

Then she saw Jared. Freshly showered and clean-shaven, he'd also dressed for dinner. His khaki pants were paired with a deep, forest green dress shirt.

Gone was her familiar lover. Here was the wealthy sophisticate Katlyn had never quite believed could want her. Her confidence wavered. He was so gorgeous that the sight of him stole her breath.

As he opened the door and said hello, excitement churned within her. When she stepped close enough to smell his spicy aftershave and feel the heat of his big body, her hormones ran amok.

For a few long seconds they stood and stared at each other, both trying to decipher what the other was thinking and feeling. Their gazes searched carefully controlled expressions, but the contest was a draw.

Katlyn finally broke the silence. "Something smells good."

Jared ushered her into the kitchen. "Mary freezes casseroles for me sometimes. I think this one's chicken tetrazzini. It's done if you're ready to eat."

"I'm starved. Anything I can do to help?" she asked although the table was already set, and he seemed to have dinner under control.

"You can get us something to drink."

A strained silence sprang up between them while she poured glasses of iced tea and Jared filled their plates. Then he held her chair until she was seated. Having him so close staggered her breathing. It made her thank-you come out a little shaky, but she recovered her composure as soon as he took a seat across from her.

They were both hungry, so they didn't waste much time on small talk until several minutes of silence had passed. Katlyn complimented Mary's cooking. Jared promised to pass on the compliment. She asked about the ranch work, and he explained that it was on schedule since the weather had been unusually mild.

At a loss for other safe subjects, they fell silent again. When they'd satisfied most of their hunger,

Jared offered her dessert. Katlyn declined, but sipped her tea as he ate a slice of Mary's apple pie.

A new, unnerving silence fell between them, and they retreated into their emotional corners, all the more wary of another round. The final fight was as inevitable as the storm of emotions that would accompany it.

Jared refused help in clearing the table and loading the dishwasher. Katlyn didn't insist. Instead, she wandered into the living room. The lights were low and soft music played from the elaborate stereo system.

It reminded her of too many cozy evenings spent making love on the soft leather sofa and even on the plush carpet. She turned abruptly and headed back toward the kitchen. Jared met her in the doorway.

"You look ready to run away."

"I guess I am," she admitted. "It's probably better that we carry on our discussion in the kitchen."

He accurately read her thoughts. "We've made love there, too, if that's why you suddenly can't handle being in the living room."

"I didn't come to rehash our relationship," she replied softly, but firmly. "If you invited me out here in hopes of changing my mind, it won't work. I've thought a lot about moving away from Kingston, and I still believe it's the best solution."

His jaw clenched, but his reply was patient. "I don't want to argue, either. I want to show you something."

Katlyn didn't have a clue. "What can you show me that I haven't already seen? I lived here, you know."

Jared caught her hand and headed for the hallway. "Come upstairs with me."

Heat coursed up her arm. His touch felt too good, too familiar. She braced herself and began to resist. "There's nothing upstairs but bedrooms, and you promised."

"I'm not trying to seduce you. There's something upstairs you haven't seen. Something important."

Katlyn frowned, but allowed him to lead her to the staircase and then to the second floor. They paused at the door of the master bedroom, and she halted again.

"This is your parents' old room. I thought your dad was the only one who used it."

"It was my grandparents' room and then my parents', but nobody ever used it much. When Dad visits, he uses a guest room. Nobody ever liked this one much."

Still wary, but curious, Katlyn slowly followed Jared into the bedroom. She'd seen it before and couldn't blame anyone for not liking it. The furniture was too heavy and ornate, the wallpaper was an ugly gold floral pattern, and the rest of the decor was too dark for her taste. It needed some serious redecorating.

Jared urged her across the room to another door. She'd thought it was a closet, but it led to an adjoining room. He opened the door, flipped the light switch, and tugged her inside.

Katlyn's breath caught in surprise, her eyes widening as she looked around. It was a nursery. A bright, fully furnished, beautifully decorated nursery. The walls were painted a delicate cream color with a border of yellow and green trains pulling alphabet cars.

On the side of the room nearest the door there was a crib, a chest of drawers and a changing table that all looked new. There were shelves lined with books and toys that looked equally new.

She moved to the crib and touched the brightly colored mobile hanging from the headboard. There were stacks of sheets, receiving blankets and comforters in gay, nursery patterns.

The changing table was well supplied with newborn disposable diapers, baby shampoos and other layette supplies. She picked up a tiny sleeper, awed by its size and softness.

Her gaze sought Jared's, but he didn't immediately offer an explanation. He just stood back and watched as she looked around.

On the opposite side of the room, she spied a big hardwood rocking chair. Beside it sat an intricately carved wooden cradle. Both were very old, but beautifully refinished.

"Oh, Jared. A cradle!"

She moved closer and touched the gleaming finish of the antique, hand-crafted cradle. "It has to be really old."

"Old, but sturdy. It's solid walnut, and it's been in my family for four generations."

A scruffy-looking brown teddy bear was lying in the cradle. Katlyn lifted it into her arms and sat down in the rocker. She stroked what must have been a well-loved toy and set the chair to rocking. Then she leveled her gaze on Jared.

"How? How did . . ." she started, stopped, and

started again. "You couldn't have done all this since last night."

Jared shook his head negatively. "It's been more than five years now."

"You hired a decorator?"

"I had the time back then, so I did the shopping and remodeling myself."

Katlyn stroked a hand over the top of the cradle. "You refinished this, too?" *Why and for whom?* she wanted to ask, but held her tongue so that he could explain in his own fashion.

"Yeah. The surface was in pretty bad shape, but it was solid, so I stripped it and did the refinishing. It wasn't hard. It just took some time."

He moved to stand beside the crib and set the mobile twirling. He had a lot of explaining to do, but was obviously having trouble finding the right words.

Katlyn noted the tension in his body, and prayed he would share his feelings. She waited patiently, knowing that his explanation could affect their whole relationship.

"I was involved with a woman a few years back," he began.

His admission caused an unexpected wave of panic to threaten Katlyn's composure. She almost told him she didn't want to hear, yet not knowing the details was more unsettling.

"It was at the end of our senior year at college. Neither of us was ready for a commitment," he continued quietly, "but then she got pregnant."

Katlyn's chest constricted as she sucked in a harsh breath. She'd known he had other lovers, yet knowing another woman had carried his child hurt more than she could have imagined.

"Her parents had planned a trip to Europe as a graduation gift, and she didn't want to disappoint them. So, we decided she should go while I came back home and got things ready for the baby. Then we'd marry as soon as she got back."

"Who was she?"

Her pulse pounded so loudly in her ears that her voice sounded weak and distant, even to her. She was afraid to hear the rest of the story. What had happened to his baby?

"Her name was Caroline, but you wouldn't know her. She wasn't from around here."

Jared paced the room and then went to the window and stared into the darkness. When he didn't continue explaining, Katlyn prompted him with another question.

"What happened?"

"She picked up some kind of viral infection and almost died while she was overseas."

The thudding of her pulse in her ears grew louder. "The baby?" she whispered.

"He didn't make it."

Jared's tone was hard and flat, devoid of emotion. He sounded totally unaffected by the tragedy. But this nursery hadn't been created by someone who didn't care. There was pride and love and caring in every tiny detail of the room. Her heart ached for the young, hopeful man he'd been five years ago.

She thought of the hours he must have spent shopping, and those spent slowly and painstakingly bringing the cradle back to its original beauty.

What sort of dreams had inspired him while he

worked? Dreams of a son who'd follow his every step or of a little girl who adored her daddy? It hurt her to know how those dreams had been shattered.

"So you called off the wedding?"

His tone took on a sharper edge. "Not right away. Caroline's mother thought they should wait until after the wedding to tell me she'd lost the baby."

Katlyn's eyes rounded in shock. "They didn't tell you about the baby as soon as it happened?"

"Not for three more weeks. Her mother would have kept it a secret until after the wedding, but Caroline finally lost her nerve and confessed everything."

No wonder he was so cynical about marriage, thought Katlyn. Not only had his parents' and grandparents' marriages failed, but his personal experience had been abysmal, too.

Her hand went to her stomach. She was already feeling protective, making plans, thinking endlessly about the baby. Jared had spent several weeks preparing for his first child. He must have been devastated.

"I'm so sorry." That was all she knew to say.

Their gazes met and locked. "Are you really?" he asked, turning and moving slowly closer.

"Sorry enough to give me a second chance to be a father? A real father? Not just a part-time parent who lives a thousand miles away?"

Katlyn's heart pounded against the wall of her chest with alarming force. Her hands trembled as she slowly and carefully laid the teddy bear back in the cradle, stalling for time. How could she make such an important decision when she could barely cope with her conflicting emotions?

Jared wanted this baby. Maybe as much as she did. She hadn't even considered the possibility. He'd already lost one child. He had a void in his life to fill, and he obviously wasn't going to let her leave without a fight.

He'd already accumulated all the basic necessities she hadn't had time to worry about yet. There was everything here a newborn would need.

He had so much to give a child. A proud heritage, a vast estate, and everything money could buy. Instead of being pleased by the fact, it scared her. Material wealth wasn't all-important. It didn't mean he could nurture their child any better than she could.

"I'll think about staying in Kingston," she finally conceded. There was so much at stake for both of them, and she needed more time to consider her options.

His eyes met hers, his features taut and gaze intent. "Think about marriage. I don't want our child labeled a bastard any more than you do."

Katlyn's eyes rounded. She'd thought about marriage. A lot. She wanted it desperately, but on her own terms. She didn't want Jared to offer marriage strictly because of the baby. She wanted him to want her, too. She wanted a lifetime commitment.

A storm of powerful feelings raged inside her. Her nerves were raw, and she couldn't stand much more pressure. The increased tension and his demand spurred a quicksilver mood change. Suddenly, she was angry and resentful.

"I would marry you, Jared, but I won't tolerate any disrespect. I won't become another despised King wife accused of trapping a rich husband. And

I won't abandon my child. Ever. So don't ask me to marry you in hopes that I'll eventually disappear like your mother."

Jared's lips thinned with anger as she spoke, a sure sign that he didn't like what he was hearing, but Katlyn didn't care. "And I won't be held responsible for every wrong a woman has ever done you."

"If we get married, we start with a clean slate," he vowed in a rough voice. "You have my word on it."

"And you won't resent having to marry?"

"I'm the one doing the proposing," he reminded her. "I'm not suggesting it'll be easy, but I wouldn't be asking if I didn't think we can make a go of it."

It was the best she could hope for at this stage. He was honest, and as long as she had his respect, there was hope of building a lasting relationship. But she had to think of the baby first.

"There's one other thing."

He stiffened. "What?"

"Before I agree to marry you, I'd want a prenuptial agreement."

Jared's brows rose in surprise, then furrowed in a deep frown. Katlyn couldn't tell if he was offended or not.

"I have no problem with a prenup. My lawyer can draft one that protects our individual assets," he said.

"I'm not worried about financial assets."

His frown deepened. "Then what is it you want?"

"I want your promise, in writing, that you'll never try to take this baby away from me. That you'll relinquish any legal right to custody."

"Like hell!" he roared. All the emotion he'd been carefully controlling was vented in one harshly expelled breath. He swore again, turned on his heel and began to pace the room. She watched as he ran a frustrated hand across the back of his neck, then turned to her again.

"What kind of a man do you think I am? How can you ask for something like that?" he charged. "It's like asking me to deny the baby is mine."

Katlyn's insides were quaking, but she remained firm. "You're a great deal wealthier than I'll ever be. I know that your name and reputation carry a lot of weight in this community. If I stay, even as your wife, I want a guarantee that you'll never use that power to take my child away from me."

Jared strode back to her, grasped her by the arms and lifted her from the chair. His grip was firm, but not painfully tight. His eyes blazed with anger and resentment. Katlyn felt him trembling with the force of his emotion, yet she wasn't alarmed.

"How can you even think it?"

His tone was rough and edged with hurt. For just an instant, she felt guilty. Then she reminded herself how much was at stake.

"You told me once that you were willing to do whatever it took to protect your birthright," she reminded gently. "I couldn't really understand that emotion until now. This baby is mine to protect, and I'm not willing to take any chances either."

Jared released her and took a step back, but his gaze remained locked with hers. "The baby is *ours* to protect," he corrected. "*Ours*—not just yours. We can protect him better as husband and wife."

"Then you'll sign a legal agreement?"

His jaw was clenched so tight that Katlyn thought it might snap. She was quivering; her knees weak, but she didn't back down on her demand.

After a few strained minutes of silence and more restless pacing, he spoke again.

"I'll have my lawyer draw up the papers. I assume it's all right to include a clause that gives me full guardianship should something happen to you."

"As the baby's father, that would be automatic."

"Not if I sign away my rights."

Katlyn hadn't considered that angle. "I don't expect you to sign away all rights to guardianship, I just want a guarantee that you won't ever sue for full custody."

Jared nodded sharply, his attitude dismissive. Katlyn didn't think she'd ever seen him look so hard, cold or unforgiving. She knew her lack of faith in him had wounded at least his pride. She felt badly about it, but didn't see any better way to handle their situation at the moment.

"As soon as I can get the papers drawn up, I'll call you and we can make the rest of the arrangements."

Katlyn was already halfway to the door. There was no sense delaying her departure. His cool, aloof tone stung. It wasn't exactly her dream of an ideal marriage plan, but she guessed that was the price for enjoying a honeymoon before the nuptials.

Jared followed her downstairs, through the house, and out the back door. They made their way in silence. There didn't seem to be anything else to say. He opened and closed her car door after a brief exchange of goodbyes, then watched as her tail-lights faded into the darkness.

A white-hot fury spread through his veins. Damn. Damn her for not trusting him. Damn her for making him care too much. Damn her for always doing the unexpected; for always rattling his hard-won control.

She hadn't been the least concerned with monetary issues or the value of what they already owned as individuals. She didn't seem to want him, his wealth or the prestige of becoming the next Mrs. King. All that apparently faded in significance when compared to their unborn child.

An aching desire for that child had hit him hard. He'd thought he'd buried those old dreams for good, but the news of Katlyn's pregnancy had resurrected them all—every painful one of them.

He knew it wasn't wise to care too much, to allow himself to dream again. His sanity wouldn't survive another loss like that. He couldn't bear another blow, even temporarily.

At this point, he'd sign whatever it took to convince Katlyn to marry him. They could iron out the rest of their problems later. Right now, he just wanted to ensure that she didn't run and hide.

Eleven

As early as possible the next morning, Jared called his lawyer, Ben Tyler. Ben, an old friend of the family, greeted him warmly.

"Hey, Jared, I'm glad you called. I have some more good news for you.

"What's that?"

"Seems your ex-stepmother has landed herself another wealthy husband. Between the judge's threats and her new spouse, she should be out of your hair permanently."

"Good riddance."

Ben chuckled. "My sentiments exactly. Now what can I do for you? I don't expect this is a social call."

Jared came right to the point. "I've decided to get married, and I'd like you to draw up a prenuptial agreement."

"Hey! Congratulations! She must be quite a lady if you're tempted to take the big leap."

Jared thought about Katlyn. She *was* quite a lady. He couldn't help but wish things were less strained between them. He had to find a way to make things right again.

"Thanks, Ben, but the lady isn't too thrilled. She's pregnant and doesn't want to get married."

There was a pause and short silence.

"Hmm, that complicates things a little. I take it you're happy about the baby?"

"I want her and the baby." His tone left no doubt about sincerity.

"Well, then, congratulations again. How do you figure I can help?"

"I want you to draw up a prenup that gives her custody of the baby."

This time there was a shocked silence, then protests. "Whoa, there. Am I hearing this right? You want marriage and the baby, but you're willing to sign away rights to claim your own child? It doesn't make sense."

"All I want is a contract that legally forbids me to file a custody suit against Katlyn. I don't want to sign away all parental rights."

"I see. It's beginning to make sense. She's afraid that you'll sue for custody if the marriage breaks up."

"Right."

"And you're willing to sign a prenup to relieve her mind?"

"Right."

"Okay, that should be simple enough. Now what about the property? Is she willing to sign away rights to your assets?"

"I don't want any mention of assets in the contract. It's strictly about the baby."

Ben hesitated, then warned him of all the inherent risks. He reminded Jared of the past few years of legal battles. Then he advised him not to follow through with his plans until he'd given the prenuptial more thought.

Jared had already considered all the angles.

Katlyn doesn't trust me. The knowledge was eating away at him night and day. He knew the risks, but he had to do something to earn her trust again.

"I want you to draw up the agreement just as if Katlyn was your client instead of me."

Ben grumbled some more, but finally agreed. He asked for details about Katlyn's name and address, then said, "I'll get on it right away and fax a preliminary copy for approval in a couple hours."

"Thanks, Ben."

Jared hung up the phone and headed back outside to work. The weather was turning colder every day, but all the cattle had been moved to their winter pastures. Now he and his men were winterizing the ranch buildings and vehicles, trying to get everything prepared for the first snowstorm of the season.

Today, more than most, he pushed himself to the limits of physical exertion. He hoisted bales of hay, climbed on roofs and wrestled with heavy equipment. He welcomed the strain of muscles and demands on his time, but nothing could stop his mind from playing one haunting refrain.

She doesn't trust me. Acknowledging that was the hardest thing he'd ever done. Somehow, he felt sucker-punched and practically powerless to fight back.

It hurt. Really hurt, deep down inside him. Katlyn didn't trust him, and that wounded him more than anything he'd ever known. He was an honest, hardworking man. And he was a fair man with integrity and principles. So why didn't she understand that he'd do what was right by her and their baby?

He understood her wariness where marriage was

concerned, but this was different. This was about
his personal integrity. She wanted legal proof that
he wouldn't try to take the baby from her.

She doesn't trust me!

The refrain just kept on going inside his head,
relentlessly, until his nerves were raw. By the time
they'd finished work for the day, he felt an overwhelming anxiety.

He entered the house with relief, but the heavy
weight of silence didn't improve his mood. He
missed Katlyn; her smile, her scent, her presence.
The ache for her was beyond physical. It scared
him, and there wasn't much that scared him anymore.

He'd already decided to go to the restaurant for
supper, so he shaved, took a quick shower and
pulled on some clean clothes. Before leaving, he
checked his office to see if Ben had faxed the document as he'd promised. Katlyn would be working,
so they could go over it together.

The fax was waiting for him. The light was blinking on his answering machine, so he punched the
button while he glanced over the prenuptial agreement.

Trudy's voice took him by surprise, and her anxious tone snared his attention.

"Jared, it's Trudy Sanders. Katlyn got terribly sick
at the restaurant, and we called for the emergency
squad. They've rushed her to the hospital. I'm on
my way there now, but thought you'd want to
know."

Click. That was all. He stared at the machine,
then checked the time of the call. It had been less
than an hour since Trudy had left the message.

A brutal, numbing fear gripped Jared. His muscles went taut for an instant, but soon jerked into action. Quickly folding the fax, he stuffed it in his pocket while racing outside to his truck. The county hospital was a half-hour's drive under normal conditions, but he could make it in a lot less.

As soon as he was on the highway, he grabbed his mobile phone and dialed information to get the hospital's number. After dialing it, he reached the hospital's receptionist who forwarded his call to the emergency department. As he expected, all they'd tell him was that Katlyn was being seen by a doctor. It was too early for them to classify her condition.

He asked to speak to Trudy, but she was conferring with the doctors. Frustration and fear ate at him as he traveled the miles between them. He had a burning need to see Katlyn, to touch her, to know she was going to be all right.

The baby. Another shock ripped through him as he remembered the baby. Was it the pregnancy making her so ill? Could she be miscarrying their child?

Would she ever forgive him if something happened to the baby? Would she blame him? He knew she was under a lot of stress, and he was responsible for a lot of it. Had it all been too much for her? He clutched the steering wheel, alternately cursing and praying that Katlyn and the baby were both all right.

She doesn't trust me! The thought plagued him as the miles rushed by. She'd stopped telling him she loved him, too.

How had something so sweet gone so sour? Was he totally at fault for having so little faith in long-term commitments? Had he destroyed her love with his refusal to acknowledge the strength of his feelings?

Katlyn doesn't trust me anymore. Was there any way to repair the damage he'd done? To renew her faith in their relationship? Would he have the chance?

Thoughts of losing her had him pressing the pedal to the floor. A mile or so from the hospital, he heard a siren and saw the flashing lights of a sheriff's cruiser, but he didn't slow down until he was pulling into the emergency room entrance.

Katlyn sat on the hospital bed, bathing her face with a cool cloth one of the nurses had provided. She tried reassuring her aunt again.

"I'm really fine now, Aunt Trudy. The doctor's just being cautious, but there's no need for you to stay. We panicked everyone at the restaurant."

"I hate leaving them so short-handed, but your health is far more important," said Trudy.

"I'd feel a whole lot better if you went back and took care of business," Katlyn teased. "Since I have to stick around here a few hours, you could come back after closing."

Her aunt started to respond, but they were distracted by a sudden explosion of voices in the outer room. The receptionist sounded insistent, and one female voice chimed in with her. A couple of male voices chorused their indignation, and yet another male voice was demanding and familiar.

"Katlyn? Katlyn?"

"Jared!" she called, her voice drawing him to the examination cubicle where she was located.

He strode in, bigger than life and totally unconcerned by the staff's attempts to detain him. His eyes were wild with anxiety as his gaze locked with hers.

"Katlyn?"

As always, her pulse kicked into high gear at the sight of him. What she saw in his eyes made her heart begin to thump in a deafening rhythm. For the first time since she'd met him, his expression was totally unguarded.

She recognized the powerful emotions he could hide no longer, saw them in his eyes, in the tautness of his jaw and the tension in his mouth. Recognized them because they represented a depth of emotion she'd only hoped he was capable of feeling.

His distress was so obvious that she found herself wanting to comfort him. She tried to give him a reassuring smile, but her face was still a little stiff.

"Jared, I'm sorry," Trudy said. "I totally forgot that I called you. I should have called back and told you Katlyn was all right."

He shook his head in response, but didn't speak. His gaze roamed over Katlyn from head to toe as though he needed to reassure himself.

"I'm fine, Jared."

When he still didn't speak, Trudy thoughtfully offered them some privacy.

"Now that Jared's here, I think I will go on back to the restaurant. You don't mind getting Katlyn home, do you?"

He still didn't speak, but nodded affirmation.

Trudy gave Katlyn a kiss on the cheek, told them goodbye and left the room.

Jared moved closer to the bed and Katlyn reached

out a hand to him. He grasped it tightly, as if reassuring himself that she was actually alive.

"I'm sorry I caused such a stir." She found herself wanting to do or say something to ease the strain on him. She'd never seen him look so ravaged with worry.

"What happened?" he asked gruffly.

"I had an allergic reaction to something. It might have been shellfish. I've never had any problem before, so I didn't know what in the world was happening. My eyes and throat both started swelling. By the time the squad got there, I could barely see or breathe."

He made a choked sound, and Katlyn hurried to reassure him. "I was fine as soon as they gave me a shot of epinephrine. I felt better within minutes."

"You'll be all right?"

"The doctor said I'll be as good as new in a couple hours, but I'll have to make sure I don't ingest any more shellfish."

"The baby?" he asked, tone gruff with concern.

Katlyn squeezed his hand in both of hers. "The baby's fine. I was never without oxygen and the doctor says the baby wasn't at risk. He wants me to stay here another hour or so, but that's strictly as a precaution."

Jared slid one hand to her stomach. The warmth penetrated her thin slacks and her muscles contracted beneath his fingers.

"I'm sorry you had such a scare," she whispered.

"I'll survive as long as you and the baby are okay. Your eyes are still red and swollen. When I first saw you, I thought you'd been crying. I thought maybe you'd lost the baby."

His voice was so tight with strain that Katlyn's chest constricted. She tugged him closer. That small tug was all it took. He swiftly wrapped his arms around her and dragged her close to his chest. For a long minute, they just held each other, drawing comfort from the contact.

She felt humbled by the tremor that shook his body, and hugged him tighter. Hope as bright as a new dawn blossomed within her.

"We're okay," she whispered. "We're both okay. I promise. The doctor swore the baby wasn't hurt. He said sometimes women are more prone to allergic reactions when they're pregnant. It was just a freak attack."

Jared finally eased his grip on her, and stepped back a little. He searched her face, then reached out and caressed her cheek with a finger.

"You're sure?"

"Yes."

"Do you hurt anywhere?"

"No. I swear. Even if I do look terrible." She knew her face was still red and a little swollen.

"You look fine," he insisted, stroking her face. "You're always beautiful."

Katlyn felt a rush of pleasure. "You think?"

"I know."

The confidence was returning to his voice, and she smiled. She patted the bed and shifted a little so that he could sit beside her. He obliged her, then grasped both her hands again.

A sweet warmth invaded Katlyn. Jared needed the physical contact. He was a very physical man and his actions sometimes spoke louder than words. She knew he needed an actual connection with her.

"You look tired."

"We spent the day winterizing the barn and loading the last cutting of hay into the barns."

"Were you coming into the restaurant?"

"Yeah, I must have been in the shower when Trudy called. I came as soon as I could."

"Did you drive too fast?"

That made his mouth tilt in a wry grin. "The sheriff, uh, escorted me for a while. He would have given me a ticket, but I told him you were here and he let me off with a warning."

Katlyn searched his face. "I'm sorry you were so frightened about the baby. I still haven't told Trudy, so she didn't understand how it would affect you."

"She knows I care about you. I didn't think about the baby until I was on my way in here. It scared me, but not as much as the thought of losing you."

His voice had gone low and deep and intimate. Katlyn's heart quickened at the sincerity in his tone and expression. His whole demeanor reflected a rare expression of vulnerability and caring.

Katlyn gripped his hands tighter. "I love you," she whispered, the words slipping out of their own volition.

Jared immediately tensed and his expression became guarded. "Do you?" he asked. "You haven't said so for a while."

"I didn't think you wanted to hear the words."

He reached into his back pocket and pulled out a sheet of paper, handing it to her.

"Do you love me enough to marry me? I had my lawyer draw up the agreement you wanted. It's pretty basic. All it says is that I won't ever sue for custody of the baby."

Katlyn glanced at the paper, but could hardly see the words because of the tears forming in her eyes. She'd demanded proof of his honorable intentions, and he'd supplied it. Now she was feeling really greedy. She wanted more. She set the paper aside and grasped his hands again.

"There's something else I'd like before I promise to marry you."

Jared's eyes narrowed, and she felt the tension radiating from him again.

"What?" he asked warily.

"I'd like to know that you have some feelings for me besides physical desire."

He relaxed a little. "I want you and need you, if that's what you mean. I don't know how I can prove that."

It was difficult to talk and hold her breath at the same time, so Katlyn forced herself to breathe.

"Do you mind answering a few questions?" she asked.

"Like what?" He was genuinely confused.

"I was just wondering if your house seemed empty without me. Do you miss me now that I'm not there every day?"

"Yes."

"Do you find yourself thinking of me at odd times of the day and night? Thinking of things you want to tell me about or share with me?"

"Yeah."

"Do you like the way I smell?" She blushed, but forced herself to continue. "I mean, do you recognize me by scent? Not just perfume, but just me?"

"I like the way you smell," he insisted, still confused by the direction of her questions. "I like the way you look and smell and feel. You know that."

"I often wondered if you really like me. The real me, not just the lover. Do you like the way I walk and talk and think? Do you admire me for my accomplishments and respect the person I am?"

Jared's gaze roamed her face. She felt the impact of his scrutiny, but didn't so much as blink. His response was incredibly important to her.

"I like all of you. The whole package. Is that what you need to know?"

"Just one more thing," she promised with a shy smile. She searched his features as closely as he'd been searching hers.

"When you see me, do you feel a wild little thrill? Does your pulse accelerate? Does my touch create an even bigger yearning? A need that's more than physical?"

Her voice had dropped to a whisper, but she didn't doubt that he heard every word. That he welcomed the confession of her love. That he knew what she was asking.

"I've never been good with words," he replied in a quiet, steady voice. "But that's a pretty good description of how I feel about you."

He slipped his hands around her waist and drew her closer. Katlyn's hands trembled as she cupped his strong face in her palms.

"It's called love, you know," she whispered on a satisfied sigh. "All those feelings? They have a name. It's called love."

Jared cocked a brow arrogantly, but a slow smile curved his mouth. "Is that right? You're an expert?"

Katlyn returned his smile with her own tremulous

one. "That's how it is for me. I don't have a lot of experience, but I'm guessing it could be like that for you, too."

"I've just been too stubborn and simpleminded to recognize the signs?" he suggested smoothly.

Her eyes lit with happiness, and her voice was teasing. "I think I'd better plead the fifth on that one, and not incriminate myself. It might not be a good idea to tell my future husband that he's stubborn and simpleminded."

"Katie!" he groaned huskily, pulling her closer to capture her mouth with a long, hungry kiss.

Katlyn tightened her grip on him. She was equally needy, so she met the demand of his lips and tongue without reservation.

Jared loved her. She'd seen it in his eyes and in his actions. Maybe he wasn't comfortable with the words. Maybe he didn't know much about the emotion, but she had no doubt that he felt deeply about her and the baby. It was more than enough to build a marriage on.

When they finally ended the kiss, Jared held her close to his heart. He nuzzled her neck and whispered in her ear. "So this is love."

A shiver of pleasure danced down Katlyn's spine. His words stole her breath, but she managed to reply. "Yeah. The real thing."

ABOUT THE AUTHOR

Becky Barker has been reading and writing romances since grade school. She saw her first book published in 1987 and has written for Dell Candlelight, Meteor Kismet, Silhouette Intimate Moments and Zebra Precious Gem Romances. This is her sixth "Gem." She hopes it brings a few hours of carefree happines to readers. She also welcomes letters at P.O. Box 113, Mt. Sterling, OH 43143 or email at: Bekybarker@aol.com.

The author has been married more than a quarter century to a former Marine who helped her create three beautiful, intelligent children. She considers herself blessed by a life filled with music, laughter, and love.